A PEACE OFFERING

A M/M HOLIDAY ROMANCE

A CRAFTY TALE

R.L. MERRILL

COPYRIGHT

First Edition 2019 Dreamspinner Press
Second Edition 2020 Celie Bay Publications LLC

Printed in the United States of America

A PEACE OFFERING

By R.L. Merrill

Dover Billings has sold his handcrafted wares at the Dickens Fair in San Francisco for over twenty years. He's not as outgoing as the other artisans at this yearly Victorian celebration and prefers to observe the festivities from the shadows. That is until a new corset maker moves into the booth next door and unsettles his carefully constructed life. Landry Malcolm is handsome, well dressed, and the life of the party... one Dover wants no part of. Too bad he's attracted to his confident younger rival.

Landry desperately wishes to get through to the beautiful artist next door, but every move he makes seems to be the wrong one, until a drunken kiss breaks through Dover's serious demeanor. Miscommunications plague any attempts to find common ground, though, leaving Landry wondering what—if anything—he can do to make things right. Will a custom-made peace offering open the door to friendship, cooperation... and maybe more?

ACKNOWLEDGMENTS

SPECIAL THANKS

To Jennifer, Rachel, and all of the Dickens cast, many thanks. Year after year you've created a wonderful experience for families in Northern California. This story is a love letter to your hard work and dedication to your craft. Happy Christmas!

To my editor, Liz, thank you for supporting me as I attempted to write this story. I'm grateful for all of your support.

To Amy Lane... the sneak peek at your Fiction Haiku method really helped me craft the perfect story. I appreciate you sharing your wisdom with me and I'm so glad we got to hang out in New Orleans.

To Marielle, thank you for being my accountability buddy this spring as I worked frantically to finish all the stories I'd committed to, including this one. I hope we continue to cheer each other on for many WIPs to come!

To Emz, my sister in horror! Thank you so much for reading for me and for always reaching out. Someday we're going to collaborate and it will be epic!

To Vanessa, my longtime pal, thank you for entrusting your incredible home to me and the kids so I would have plenty of time and inspiration to craft this tale. I'm so grateful our friendship has endured the trials and tribulations of life and that we're growing oldish together. Not old, though. Never.

And to my husband, who is quite the craftsman, thank you so much for all of the beautiful things you've created. I hope someday you will have all the time you want to make your pens, paint your figures, or build kits with our son. You deserve it after how much you've supported me. I love you.

1

D ecember 2018
Dover

"AND THAT'S A WRAP! Happy Christmas, everybody!"

Champagne bottles popped among whoops and hollers from the booth next to Dover Billings. He was too tired to do more than roll his eyes. The Great Dickens Christmas Fair and Victorian Holiday Party had lasted five weekends this year, and Dover was wrecked. Bah humbug, for real.

The new guy with all the fancy corsets next door had driven him crazy the entire run of the fair. Dover had suffered from endless bawdy tunes, the wall being constantly bumped by the new guy's rowdy friends, and several times his drunken patrons had even knocked over one of Dover's displays, breaking two of his acrylic pens and a magnifying glass.

"Hey, Dover, did you hear old man Williams is retiring? You know what that means?"

Miranda Prasad, Dover's business partner, was always in the know when it came to fair gossip. He usually tried to stay out of it, but this information could benefit him.

"It means I will be requesting his spot as soon as proposals open," Dover said. "It also means I'll be asking *not* to be next door to the new guy and his shit show."

"You mean Landry? He's hilarious. Last weekend I had him fit me for a new corset. I can't wait to wear it next year."

Dover didn't even have the energy to roll his eyes once more. Miranda was married to Darwish, Dover's best friend and the bass player for their prog rock cover band, Sense of Measure. She'd been working with him at the San Francisco Dickens Fair for the past eight years, and together they sold his acrylic and wood pen sets and other implements as well as her Victorian-inspired jewelry using antique keys and other recycled items. "I can't believe you went over there. Isn't his group a little... over-the-top?"

Miranda elbowed him. "Just because they like to sing and dance and prance around in their undergarments doesn't mean they're over-the-top. You're a bit of a prude, Dover Billings."

He supposed she was right. Fair was filled with the kinds of people he'd stayed away from in school: the drama kids who turned everything into a performance. Being the son of the drama teacher meant he got enough of that at home. While he loved the stagecraft side of the theater, he shied away from acting. Dover ended up at Dickens because his father had been friends with the family who'd run the event since the 1970s. Dad had been an actor, painter, crafts-man, and lover of all the arts. Luckily those genes were passed down, and the two of them bonded over their creations. They'd sold their wares together for years until his father retired and moved to the desert with Dover's stepmother.

"Hey, you guys want some champagne?"

There he was: the object of Dover's frustration, in all his glory. Landry Malcolm was a golden boy. A successful tailor and costumer, the guy worked the Dickens Fair because it was a fun way to hang out with friends through the holidays, unlike most of the vendors who needed to make serious money during the holidays to support their art the rest of the year.

"No, thank—"

"We'd love some," Miranda cut in. She kicked Dover behind the table before coming around to the front to accept two glasses of champagne.

"I figured we could all use a glass after this hellacious schedule. It's been a blast, but *whoo*, I cannot wait to sit in front of my TV for a week and decompress."

The guy's smile even sparkled, if that were a thing. He'd dressed in the finest period wear throughout the show, changing into different outfits sometimes even twice or three times a day. At this moment his shirt and vest were unbuttoned, showing off his tanned chest. Landry was younger than Dover, was somewhere around six feet tall, and was built like an Olympic swimmer. His blond hair was just below his jaw, and he wore his sideburns long during fair season. He looked like he'd stepped off a movie set, he was that gorgeous.

"I can't wait to see my corset." Miranda downed the last of her champagne and handed the glass back to Landry.

"Excellent. I should have it ready for you in a couple of weeks? Maybe? I'll call you when it's ready for a fitting. I'm pulling out all the stops on this one. You'll be even more smashing than usual, milady." He executed a full gentleman's bow, and Dover wanted to snort. Why did he have to be so extra? *Why do I keep staring at him like a starving man?*

Miranda squealed and hugged Landry, giving him a kiss on the cheek.

Dover turned away and made a face. All this fuss over a freakin' corset was beyond him.

"You know, I make men's corsets as well, in case you're ever in the market. I'd love to fit you for one."

Dover turned sharply to look at Landry. Was he *flirting*?

Landry had one eyebrow raised as he waited for an answer.

"I'm fine." Dover cleared his throat and looked down at his shabby vestments. He'd worn the same outfit for the past ten years. It was a bit ratty, sure, but he didn't need fancy-pants coming in here telling him he needed to dress better. "I don't like anything constricting."

Landry seemed disappointed. "Fair enough. Let me know if you change your mind. I do my best to put comfort and fashion on the same level of importance. I'd think you'd want something flexible since you're working—"

"I'm good," Dover said. He handed back the glass he hadn't sipped from. "And thanks, but I don't—"

"I'll have his, then," Miranda said, taking the glass and downing its contents. "Thank you, Landry." She slipped her arm in his and led him back toward his store. "I want to see what else you've got over there. I might want some of those stockings."

Landry smiled at her, but he glanced back at Dover with a sad expression on his face.

"See you around, Dover."

Dover waved to him, but something clenched in his chest. He hadn't meant to be rude. Okay, he was often blunt, and a lot of people took it personally. It wasn't his fault. He said what he meant and didn't believe in sugarcoating things for people. Likely the reason why he was still single at thirty-eight years old.

He went to work closing up his booth, packing away his inventory that hadn't sold, which thankfully wasn't much. Being open five weekends netted him ample sales to cover his booth fee for this year, his warehouse rent for first quarter, and a little extra to stock up on supplies. He thought about Miranda's gossip from earlier. If old man Williams wasn't going to be back, Dover wanted that booth. He could bring in some of his larger pieces, maybe even his paintings, and perhaps experiment with his offerings. He did *not* want to be stuck in the corner next to the annoyingly attractive tailor for another season.

"Don't be such a dick, Dover."

"That's right, dick. He's so nice," Miranda said, catching him talking to himself as she wandered back in. "Why don't you like him?"

Dover shrugged. Because the truth was, he found him attractive, and Landry Malcolm was the kind of handsome distraction Dover didn't need.

"He's so nice. I wish you'd give him a chance."

"He *is* nice. He's young. I don't know. It's just... I don't have anything in common with him."

She raised an eyebrow. "Other than spending months together each year, celebrating your love of Victorian-inspired wares, your theater background—"

"I built sets for my dad—"

"Your obvious attraction."

Dover blinked.

"You think I didn't notice that while you were trying to appear annoyed at his antics, you couldn't take your eyes off of him?"

"I have no idea what you're talking about," he lied.

Yes, Landry Malcolm was beautiful to look at. But beautiful men were just that: lovely to gaze at from afar. Not to let into your life.

2

J*uly 2019*
Landry

LANDRY WAS EXPERIENCING a level-ten foodgasm over his chowder bread bowl from Sam's Chowder truck as he walked back to his traveling costume shop when he spotted the last person on earth he thought he'd run into on a sunny day on the San Francisco Bay.

Dover Billings was the biggest mystery Landry had come across in a long time. The man was a quiet beauty. Long, dark brown curls with faint wisps of gray flowed down his narrow back. Dover was built on the slight side, but he reminded Landry of European nobility from ages ago with his aquiline nose and big blue eyes. His pale skin likely had more to do with remaining in his workshop most days rather than exposing himself to the sun, but it was probably for the best. Landry knew his dalliances in the sun would likely land him in the dermatologist's chair for sun-damaged spot removals at a premature age. Twenty-seven wasn't too young to be thinking of these things, and yet he still loved the beach.

He stood off to the side behind a rack of antique mirrors and watched as Dover smiled—he actually smiled—at a customer. Landry had admired his handiwork during the previous winter's Dickens Fair, even sending his best friend, Gwen, over to purchase one of his fountain pens. He'd have gone himself, but he had a feeling something about him annoyed Dover. Every time he'd passed by and tried to make small talk, he got responses barely above a grumble.

Dover's coworker, Miranda, was sweet. Landry had done a little digging with her to make sure he was barking up the right tree where Dover was concerned, which she confirmed. She'd added that Dover was shy and liked to keep to himself as an explanation for Dover's standoffish behavior. Seemed like more than that to Landry, but for whatever reason, he couldn't shake his fascination with the brooding artist. Landry didn't want for the company of handsome older men, but this one was different. There was something soulful about him that drew Landry in.

The older woman who was at Dover's booth continued speaking with Dover and even had him laughing now. And blushing! Landry couldn't help himself; he had to move in closer to eavesdrop.

"I still remember the look on Darwish's face when I told him his bowl cracked in the kiln. He was heartbroken. 'No, Mrs. Ramirez! I can't fail ceramics! My parents will kill me. They never wanted me to waste my time on art classes. Oh! I'm sorry, I didn't mean your class.' Always having to extract his foot from his mouth."

Dover chuckled, his cheeks a lovely blush pink. "His parents still give him a hard time about taking art classes in high school, even after all these years. They blame me he didn't go to Harvard and instead chose to waste his time at the Academy of Art."

"But you both were so talented! Do you still paint?"

Dover shrugged. "Some. But turning wood and acrylics pays the bills, so I spend most of my time on the lathe."

Dover spotted Landry out of the corner of his eye, and the easy way he was conversing with the older lady seemed to vanish.

"How's your father? He was the best drama teacher we ever had.

Sure was sad to see him go, but then he deserved a relaxing retirement more than anyone I knew."

Landry hovered over the end of the table, running his fingers over the smooth finishes of the several styles of pens. It seemed that Dover made other things as well, such as letter openers, wine bottle stoppers, and even candle holders. Landry paused at the next display. It was a gorgeous wooden box created to look like an old-fashioned clock or radio, and the tag next to it said Bluetooth Speaker. *How clever.* Landry opened the latch, and inside, sure enough, was a small speaker.

"He's good. He and my stepmom are settled down in Indio. They like the artist vibe down there. He'll be up for Dickens, though."

"Oh, I love the Dickens Fair." The woman pressed a hand to her chest. "My wife and I used to go there every year until the boys got too old to be patient while we shopped. I loved all the period clothing they sold there."

Dover nodded in Landry's direction. "Landry here took over the corset-selling business this past year."

The woman turned to gape at him, and he bowed with grand flourish.

"Landry Malcolm at your service, milady. The finest custom vestments in town." He stood and smiled at Dover, who was still staring at him like he was the last person he'd expected to see. Maybe that wasn't a bad thing? Landry hoped a change of scenery might give them a much-needed do-over.

"Pleased to meet you. Ramona Ramirez, art teacher. I taught this young man all he knows about painting. Well, all he knew, what was it, twenty years ago?"

Dover smiled, but with less wattage than he'd had from afar, when he hadn't known Landry was watching him. "Yes, ma'am. I graduated twenty years ago."

"You paint, too?" Landry was increasingly fascinated the more he learned about Dover.

Dover shrugged. "When I can. Most of my time off work is spent making inventory for Dickens and other shows."

Landry nodded. He knew he was incredibly lucky to be doing what he loved. His tailoring business, inherited from his grandmother, was far into the black. The Dickens Fair had been an experiment this past year, and one that paid off handsomely. The endeavor netted him enough money to cover his booth and his latest exploit. He'd bought the travel trailer to take to fairs in the summer just to sell some of his passion projects as well as the corsets, but his shop did steady business, and he'd been able to hire two full-time tailors/seamstresses to handle most of their day-to-day business, giving him the time to design what he liked and work these weekend gigs. Life was good, and he was making money hand-over-fist. He knew most of the artisans at these shows weren't necessarily as fortunate.

"I'd love to see your paintings sometime." God, he sounded almost breathless. He was like a damn schoolgirl around this man. He was so in awe of Dover's talent, and that, in addition to how attractive the guy was, meant he couldn't keep his cool.

"Oh, uh—"

"There's my wife. It was nice to meet you, Landry. Dover, give an old lady a hug."

Dover came around the table in a pair of worn Levi's that looked buttery soft and hugged his lean hips lovingly. Dover embraced the woman, who couldn't have been much older than fifty. Far from an old lady in Landry's estimation.

"Thank you for coming by," Dover said, giving her one last squeeze. "I'll see what I can come up with for you."

She winked at him, gave Landry an appraising look, and then scurried off after her wife, who had a long salt-and-pepper braid down her back and was wearing a motorcycle club vest.

"That's cool she came to see you," Landry said, attempting to break the awkward silence.

"I owe her a lot. My mom died right before I started high school. Mrs. Ramirez's art classes were the only thing that kept me in school."

"I'm so sorry," Landry said, feeling that maybe he finally had a clue as to what made Dover so serious. "Was it unexpected?"

Dover looked down at the display in front of him and straightened some pens. "She had a stroke. It was totally out of the blue."

His voice faltered a little on the last bit, and Landry wished they knew each other a little more so he could give him a hug. Landry was a hugger, an all-around affectionate guy, but Dover didn't give any indication that he was okay with the physical, except for the hug from his teacher and longtime mentor.

"Strokes are so scary," Landry said. "There's just no way of knowing."

Dover cleared his throat. "So, you here as a vendor?"

Landry smiled so wide he was sure his eyes nearly disappeared. "I am! I bought an antique trailer and renovated it into a little pop-up shop. I've been experimenting with some new designs, reusing clothing and turning it into something new and fresh. The trailer has a little dressing room and racks in it. It's been a huge hit. This is my first weekend here at Treasure Island, but I took it out to the Alameda County Fair for the run, and it was a smash! I sold out of everything. Have you ever worked the county fair?"

Dover shook his head. "I can only do weekends. I work during the week."

"Oh yeah? What do you do?"

"Tech for the school district. Basically, I fix Chromebooks and hook up teacher computers to the printers every time they get kicked off the system."

"Oh, wow, computers, too?"

"Yeah." Dover's cheeks reddened faintly. He seemed resistant to talking about himself.

"Is there anything you don't do?"

"I can't cook very well. I hate it, actually."

Now he was getting somewhere. Landry had learned more about Dover in this exchange than in the months they'd prepared for Dickens, and he really liked what he saw. "Cooking is tough, especially when you're trying to fit it in between work and art. Do you at least have a shop where you live, or are you renting space?"

Dover shook his head, and a breeze caught his long locks,

blowing them in his face. As he spoke, he pulled a hair tie from his wrist and tied it back. Landry was so fascinated with the movements, he almost lost what Dover said.

"Yeah, no. I live in a town house, and the neighbors complained about the noise. I rented a space in a warehouse, but then after the Ghost Ship fire, the manager kicked a bunch of us out, said we were a fire hazard. I ended up renting Miranda's garage. Her husband is my best friend. They had a two-car detached garage in their backyard in Castro Valley, so he said I could move my shit over there. It's a little out of the way, but it's better than what I had." He chuckled. "Pissed Miranda off, though. We had to move our band equipment into the house to make room for my studio. Now we practice in the living room and she has no place to hide."

"Man," Landry said, hating that Dover couldn't pursue his art without obstacles. "I'm glad you found a place, though. That's tough. But wait. A band too?"

"Yeah. Prog rock cover band. I play guitar." Dover shrugged and busied himself tidying up his space.

"That's so cool. I don't know much of that music. Like, Rush?"

"Yeah. Rush is the main one people think of. We play some Pink Floyd, Yes, and Dream Theater. Some newer stuff like Baroness and Coheed and Cambria."

"I'll have to check them out," Landry said, trying to mentally record the names he'd never heard before. "I sing in a choir, but mostly we sing show tunes or the classics. Do you guys play anyplace local?"

"Yeah. A few bars around the East Bay. Nothing major. We mostly do it for fun and because we love the music."

Landry tried to work up the nerve to ask him out, thinking maybe, just maybe, they'd turned a corner. He decided to stick with a safe topic. Or rather, one he thought was safe. "Hey, so I want to bring back the windows this year, at Dickens. Some of the cast said they thought they were so much fun and assured me they'd be a draw."

The "windows" consisted of a booth with plexiglass that resembled a store front display. Throughout the day actors performed short vignettes in the booth through a series of choreographed movements similar to a live-action mannequin display at a department store. When the previous corset maker left, the fair was without the windows for a couple of seasons. Landry thought bringing back this favorite attraction would be a great idea.

Dover scoffed. "The windows? Yeah, they're a draw. They're also a pain in the ass."

"Really? Why do you think so?"

Dover exhaled and moved around to the other side of his display, fiddling with the wine stoppers in a bowl, making sure the designs were all visible. They were all different colors and textures of wood. So elegant.

"They sort of bring an element to that part of the fair that is distracting."

Did he really feel that way? "They do draw in more customers for all of the vendors in that bay, though. Don't you think?"

Dover didn't answer. *Shit.* Obviously, this was not the way to get Dover to loosen up.

"I was going to ask some of the cast to model for me." *It's now or never.*

Dover nodded, but he didn't look up. "Good luck with that. You'll probably find plenty. The actors who do the Naughty French Postcards show would do it. Probably a lot of customers, too."

His words were encouraging, but this didn't seem to be the time to ask him if *he* would model. Truthfully, Landry didn't know how well he'd handle dressing Dover. He'd developed such a crush on the guy at this point, he was perilously close to embarrassing himself. "I'm really looking forward to it. I put in for Mr. Williams's booth. At least that way I'll be out of your hair. I know some of my customers got a little overzealous."

This time, Dover did look at him. Pointedly. "I put in for it too."

"Oh," Landry said, inwardly cursing. The last thing he needed was one more reason for Dover to dislike him. "Well, either way, I'll do my best to keep my patrons under control."

"Yeah. I'd like to not lose any more merchandise." He turned away and busied himself with his inventory, his eyebrows nearly meeting in the middle. Landry took that as his wish to end the conversation, and that made him incredibly sad.

"I'm sorry about that. I should have offered to pay. I'll, um, let you get back to work. I just wanted to say hello."

"Yeah. Thanks for coming by." At least he made eye contact this time, but there was nothing welcoming in his tone.

"See you, soon, I hope."

Dover nodded and turned back around, leaving Landry to walk away like a wounded puppy.

Ugh. He hated feeling that way, but he'd so gotten his hopes up when he'd seen Dover's booth. Somehow, someway, Landry hoped he and Dover could at least be friends. He wanted more than that, but he'd settle for civility with the mysterious man.

3

O*ctober*
Dover

"GOD, I really hope we get that booth."

Dover was anxious as he and Miranda rode in her Prius to the all-hands meeting. Dover's truck was in the shop. Again. It had been a frustrating couple of weeks as his truck broke down, his lathe had given up the ghost, and his last order of acrylics was late, meaning he was going to be behind in finishing the pens he was making for Dickens.

"It would be nice to have that extra space," Miranda said. "I love the new speakers and amplifiers you're bringing. What a great idea."

"Yeah, they're super easy to build, and I know there are plenty of music enthusiasts who swing through Dickens. I sold as many as I brought to each of the shows this summer."

"Yeah, I'm sorry I couldn't go with you." Miranda rubbed a hand over her growing belly.

"You had more important things to work on, like taking care of you and the baby."

Miranda found out in April that she was expecting, and it had been a rough first trimester for her. She'd had to take leave from work for a few weeks as she battled twenty-four-hour morning sickness.

"Yeah, well, I'm just glad that part's over. Although things are getting quite uncomfortable."

She wasn't due until January, so she'd worked diligently on her jewelry, determined to work Dickens Fair with him in spite of her condition.

"If you keep growing, we're going to absolutely need the bigger booth or else we won't fit."

"Thanks a lot," she said, elbowing him, though she laughed. She'd had a great sense of humor about the whole thing. Darwish was in awe of how strong and brave she was. Dover was ecstatic for his best friends.

"If we don't get the bigger booth, it'll be okay. We did great last year! We made more money than the last two years."

"Yeah, but if I can't get the damn lathe fixed, I'm going to have to make enough to buy a new one."

"I'm so sorry, Dover. I know it's been frustrating for you. Can't your dad loan you the money?"

"There's no way I would ask him. I can't afford to overextend myself, and if I couldn't pay him back, I'd be devastated. He and Hillary have a good thing going in the desert and need all of their investments to carry them through retirement."

Miranda reached over and patted his knee. "You're a good son, Charlie Brown. I totally borrowed money from my mom to buy new tools this year. She considers herself a silent partner in my business."

Dover chuckled. Miranda was younger than Dover and Darwish by about eight years, and her mother was a bit of a trophy wife to Miranda's CEO stepfather. "She's also a walking advertisement. I've seen her wearing not only your earrings and necklace combos, but also rings on, like, all of her fingers and bracelets on both wrists... plus your screen-printed T-shirts."

"Yeah, she gets carried away sometimes, but it's nice having your mom be your biggest fan. Oh, shit, Dover. I'm so sorry."

Dover smiled. "It's okay. My mom was my biggest fan. My dad's a close second."

Miranda turned to face him at the next red light. "And she's smiling down on you now. Everything is going to come together for you, I promise."

They parked as close to the restaurant as they could get and walked over. Others from the cast of Dickens Fair arrived at the same time, and there were hugs all around. Miranda took off with some of the women who were actors in Dickens Family Parlor, and Dover found a seat off in a corner so he could watch everyone else. He wasn't exactly antisocial, but he didn't know how to play the game, so he didn't try. If people thought he was rude, so be it. There were enough people in the Dickens regulars who he'd known for years and who he knew were friends. They respected him.

A server came by, and he ordered an old-fashioned for him and a Shirley Temple for Miranda. He waved to a few friends, and several came by to give him hugs.

A raucous burst of laughter echoed across the restaurant. Dover scanned the room and wasn't surprised to find Landry and the two women who'd worked the booth with him last year, Gwen and Trudy, seated beside him. He was dressed in a three-piece suit complete with spats. Dover glanced down at his flannel shirt and black skinny jeans and sighed. Even if he wanted to dress nice, he didn't have the funds for a wardrobe like Landry's. Of course, he probably made all his own suits, but still.

Landry. *Damn.* Dover had been thrown when Landry came to visit his booth at the Treasure Island festival over the summer. It was strange to see people from Dickens in other places, although there were a few other vendors he saw at events, especially the Scottish Games at the end of the summer. But Landry had been so *nice* to him, and Dover had been, well... he'd kind of been a jerk. He was shocked when Landry mentioned he'd put in for the bigger booth as well, but it made sense. Landry's booth did so much business during fair last year, he'd been the talk of the Cow Palace back barns, where Dickens was held every year. But unlike Dover, who depended on his sales at fair to keep his art in business, Landry was doing pretty damn well, from what he'd heard.

Yeah, he'd snooped. He'd asked Miranda about Landry's shop after she went to be fitted for her corset. She was so pissed she wouldn't be able to wear it this year now that she had a baby belly. She'd modeled it for him, and Darwish and Dover had been incredibly impressed by the beautiful garment. Landry had promised her he'd make her something amazing, and he'd delivered. Dover had even driven by his shop near the Rockridge BART station in Oakland and had been impressed. He didn't dare go inside, though, especially after how he'd spoken to Landry during the summer. It was just as well. A guy like Landry wouldn't ever give someone like Dover a second glance. He was being nice; that was the only reason he'd come by over the summer, although at one point, Dover had thought maybe he was flirting. Not that Dover was really good at picking up those kind of things. He wasn't the guy people flirted with, unless it was his female friends. They knew he was safe, and their overtures were harmless.

"All right, all right, pipe down everyone. Welcome to the 2019 Dickens Family Christmas Fair Season. Belinda will be coming around to hand you your information packet, complete with a map and schedule for the season. If there are questions, you can speak to us after the meeting. Now, a few announcements...."

Dover tuned out as soon as he saw Belinda coming around with the packets.

Please let me have the Williams booth. Please let me have the Williams booth.

Belinda started on the other side of the room, and Dover watched as Landry received his. The two women he was with both looked over his shoulder and squealed at the contents of the packet. Landry smiled and exhaled as though he was relieved. None of this boded well for Dover.

"Whatever happens, it's going to be fine." Miranda slid into the seat next to his with a little difficulty. "Oooo! A Shirley Temple? I love Shirley Temples!"

Dover couldn't stop staring in Landry's direction, as though he could somehow, through telepathy, find out what had Landry smiling like that.

And then Landry caught his eye.

His smile seemed to convey sympathy.

"Fuck," Dover growled under his breath. Well, at least they wouldn't be right next to each other again. If he got Williams's old booth, he'd be in the center of the bay, smack-dab in the center of all the action.

If Dover took his own interests out of the equation, it really made the most sense for Landry to have that booth. It would be the easiest place to set up the windows, like he'd mentioned he'd wanted to do when they met up in the summer. It just stung. Depending on which booth he received, he may or may not have the space to add some new merchandise. Depending on where his booth was located, he might be forced to watch the windows—and Landry—the entire run of the season.

Dover had worked his father's booth in high school and college for extra cash and to spend time with the man who was his every-thing. He'd wandered past the windows several times a day and stopped to gaze at the actors. Most of the time there would be women posed in various stages of undress. He'd been fascinated by their garments, and lack thereof. But it had been the men he'd gone back to see again and again.

One of the actors back then actually reminded him a lot of Landry: blond, handsome, well-dressed, and well-mannered. Exactly Dover's cup of tea. The last weekend of the show—it must have been Dover's sophomore or junior year in high school—he'd gone by the windows several times during the day, his excuse being that it was the fastest way to the bathrooms, even though that wasn't exactly true. The blond man, probably in his twenties, had been in the booth each time, and with a different man or woman. As Dover walked by that last time, the man made eye contact with him... and winked. Dover had been so shocked he'd stopped walking and stared. The man's wickedly handsome smile had done things to his insides, things he had only recently begun to understand. He'd been close to fifteen before he started to have the stirrings of sexuality, and they'd been solely in the presence of men. Seeing this particularly handsome man clad only in trousers and a corset vest while smoking a pipe took his breath away and was the source of his fantasies for months after the season ended. The next season, the man hadn't returned. Dover eventually developed a habit of bedding pretty men, which never proved wise in the morning light.

Belinda finally made it to his table, and Miranda reached for the packet. She immediately flipped to the map, then sighed.

"I already know," he said when she started chewing on her lip.

"I'm sorry, Dover."

"It's fine. Really. We'll make it work. Where are we?"

She pointed on the map to the booth directly across from the booth he'd wanted. The booth Landry had had the year prior.

"We'll have more room than we did, at least," she said, trying to make the situation better.

"I know, but I had plans. Hey, take good notes for me."

She smiled at him as he stood from the table and headed toward the men's room, probably hoping he wasn't going off to sulk. He wasn't. Not totally. He simply needed a minute to breathe.

He was washing his hands at the sink and trying to regain his composure when the door opened.

Landry.

"Oh, hey. Dover, I'm sorry—"

He held up a hand. "It's fine." If he said it enough times, he might actually believe it.

"I'm okay with what I had last year. Maybe they'll let us switch."

Dover shook his head as he dried his hands on a towel. "Don't do that. You need the bigger space. It's fine."

Landry snorted and then covered his mouth. "I'm sorry. That was rude. It's just 'It's fine' sounds a helluva lot like 'Fuck you.'"

"Oh God," Dover said, laughing a bit himself. "That's not what I mean, I'm sorry."

Landry waved his hand and moved past Dover to the sinks to wash up and straighten his hair in the mirror. He looked flushed, as though he'd maybe had a few more drinks than Dover. He also smelled really good.

"Don't worry. I promise, I'll make it up to you. I'll be sure the window facing your booth will have an excellent view."

"Why? Are you planning to model?" *Oh, God, did I actually say that?*

Landry's shock was evident. Dover knew he couldn't take it back. He stood a little taller and kicked his chin out. Maybe *all* the drinks were a little strong tonight. No way he would have been brave enough to say that.

Landry's cheeks reddened further, and he dried his hands quickly. He stepped close, really close, well into Dover's personal space.

"That could be arranged. I was actually going to ask you to model. Perhaps we can pose together." His voice had taken on a breathy quality that made Dover's heart race. Heat radiated off Landry, or perhaps it was Dover's own libido coming to life, warming him from the inside out at the thought of seeing Landry in fewer clothes. But then he picked up on what Landry said.

"Me? Model? No—"

"Oh, please? Why not? It'll be fun, and you are absolutely stunning, don't you know that?"

Landry reached up and twirled a loose strand of Dover's long hair around his fingertip, a quiet moan issuing from his throat.

Dover swallowed and absently swayed closer to Landry, their chests brushing, the contact giving Dover goose bumps. "I—"

Landry closed the distance, cradled Dover's face in his soft hands, and pressed his lips to Dover's, taking him so by surprise, he groaned. He didn't pull away. He stood leaning in, memorizing the feel of Landry's soft lips—which had some sort of tingly lip balm on them—touching his own and every point of contact between them. Landry's stubble burned his skin, and Dover wanted closer, wanted to feel that burn on other places. Landry smelled like cherries, menthol, and liquor; the latter so strong it brought tears to Dover's eyes. It was enough to wake him. What the hell was he doing kissing someone, a fair-someone, in the fucking john at the all-hands meeting?

"I'm... wow.... Dover. I—"

Dover took a step back, stunned. He reached up to touch his still-tingling lips. "Excuse me."

Rather than freak out in front of the guy, Dover pushed past him and practically ran for the table he was sharing with Miranda. He slid into a chair next to her, and put his head in his hands.

"Where were you? They're already done talking about the schedule and the build weekends—"

"Sorry. Did I, uh, miss anything?"

Miranda looked at him and blinked. She leaned closer. "Why do you smell like Carmex?"

"I—never mind. Look, are you almost ready to go?"

"What's wrong, Dover? Are you okay? I know you said you were fine, and not like I believed you, but—"

"See you soon, Dover."

Miranda's jaw dropped as Landry walked by their table and winked at Dover.

"Let's go—"

"You are going to tell me what happened pronto, old man." Miranda maneuvered her way around the table and waddled toward the door, holding her back as she went.

Once they got in the car, Dover relayed what had happened in the restroom. "He only kissed me because he was drunk."

"No, no, no, Dover, my dear. That's not how it works. Alcohol lowers inhibitions—it doesn't brainwash people into doing something they didn't want to do in the first place."

"I'm sure there are people who would disagree with you."

"Yeah, but not in this scenario." She glanced at Dover out of the corner of her eye. "What did you do?"

"I'm not sure. I wasn't exactly expecting it."

"Well, did you like it?"

Dover had to think about it for a minute, which made Miranda even more impatient with him.

"I don't know! It was... unexpected. But...."

"But what? Come on! You're making me crazy over here! Were his lips soft? I need to know these things!"

"He had some sort of lip balm on."

Miranda gasped. "Carmex! I *knew* I smelled Carmex on you. He must have given you more than a peck if you smelled like him."

Dover couldn't help the chuckle that escaped. "Yeah. More than a peck, less than a French, are you satisfied?"

"The question is, are you?"

No, he wasn't satisfied. That realization happened instantly. He didn't have to think about it. Yeah, he'd practically run out on the guy, but it wasn't because he hadn't liked his kiss or hadn't wanted more, but that was the problem. Dover preferred solitude to company. He'd tried his luck with pretty faces and had never found what he'd imagined he'd want in a relationship. There was something about Landry, though. The way he smelled, the way he was so comfortable in his own skin despite his young age, and the way he seemed to really *see* Dover... as though no matter how hard Dover tried to blend into the woodwork, Landry still saw him. It was unsettling and also a little bit exciting. But then what did they even have in common besides Dickens? Not music, not personalities.... The situation felt hopeless.

But that kiss....

4

October
Landry

"YOU *STILL* LOOK like the cat who ate the canary, Landry James. Are you going to tell us what happened last night?"

Gwen, Trudy, and Landry arrived at his shop bright and early Saturday morning, ready to pack up their inventory for fair. The next weekend they'd be able to start building their booth, and the following week, they'd be moving in, so this was their last shot. The shop would be open during the week. Landry's grandmother, mother, and aunt would be helping out while he and his best girlfriends worked the lucrative holiday fair.

It was true. Despite feeling a tad hung over after the three of them had done several rounds of shots with some the other cast members, Landry hadn't been able to stop smiling. He'd gone home, fallen into bed fully clothed, and proceeded to dream about the elusive Dover Billings.

He'd followed him into the restroom with the sole purpose of apologizing to him. He'd taken one look at the man he'd fantasized about for months, and he'd acted. Dover's lips had felt like heaven; the bitter taste of scotch had made Landry crazy. He'd wanted to explore with his tongue, his hands.... Basically, he'd wanted a helluva lot more than a quick kiss in a bathroom. He just hoped it was enough to maybe get Dover thinking Landry wasn't someone to be avoided.

"I ran into Dover. And then my lips ran into his. As is common-place in a men's restroom."

Gwen squealed. "Oh! He's so cute!"

"How did he react?" Trudy asked.

Landry's smile fell a little. "I'm pretty sure I freaked him out. He kind of ran away. First time that's happened to me. It kind of makes me want him even more, is that creepy?"

His two best friends laughed hysterically, clutching their stom-achs while they gasped and barked like seals.

"He's so serious! I can only imagine he panicked."

"He kind of did." Dover had frozen for a millisecond before he'd kissed Landry back with gusto. Landry had expected perhaps a tenta-tive kiss, or even an abrupt rejection. Dover's kiss had been a welcome surprise. He had a feeling he'd only felt the tip of the pent-up passion iceberg within the quiet man.

"Are you going to message him? Maybe take him out?" Trudy had her hands full of fabric, her expression so hopeful.

"I don't know how to proceed, honestly. Do I press on, be persis-tent? Or will that scare him away even more?"

Gwen brought over a box for Trudy and helped her pack it care-fully, taking care not to rip the silk or get runs in the delicate pieces. "If you ask me, you are going to need to approach this with caution. From what I heard, Dover hardly talks to anyone except his friend Miranda, who works with him, and some of the old-timers. You know he's been doing fair since he was a teenager? His father used to play Bob Cratchit every year."

"Really? So his father was an actor and he's the quiet artist. I'm intrigued. What else do your sources tell you? Wait, are we talking about actual people sources, or from one of your readings?"

Gwen threw a tape measure at him, and he caught it in one hand. He couldn't help teasing her. He trusted Gwen's intuitions on people, but he wasn't sure he bought into her tarot reading. He needed something more tangible when it came to problem-solving.

"Don't sass me! It just so happened that last year I got to know the gals from the Dickens Family Parlor, and their director has known him for a long time. I asked about him, and she gave me the goods." She rested her hands on her hips. "You know, his mom died when he was a young teenager, maybe before high school even. Stroke, I think. Totally unexpected. He and his father were really close, but she said he had a hard time of it."

Landry unspooled the tape measure and wound it around his finger over and over. "He told me that when I saw him over the summer. It's so sad." He couldn't imagine what his life would have been like without his mom. Dad was a good man, but his mother and grandmother were his biggest fans. They supported all of his thespian dreams and his choice to follow his grandmother's footsteps and become a well-sought-after tailor and costumer. He'd worked his way up from the shop to local theater, and he'd even done a few small-budget films, with grand designs to do more. His ultimate goal would be large productions in the city or even Hollywood. It could happen. In the meantime, he enjoyed the shop and the events. He'd bought out his grandmother's business in Oakland and used his trust fund to modernize things a bit. Life was good. He was close to his family and worked with his two best friends. Maybe it was too much to hope for: finding a companion. Couldn't hurt to dream—and he'd been dreaming about Dover—but perhaps he should be satisfied with his life for once instead of reaching for that next milestone. He was only twenty-seven. There was time, even if he was an impatient bastard.

"Speaking of the Naughty Postcards show... the director's looking for a male understudy." Trudy looked pointedly at Landry.

He scoffed at her. "You think just because I am an unapologetic exhibitionist, I would jump at the chance to be in her show that I loved so much last year?" He tapped his chin with one finger. "You'd be correct!"

Trudy clapped her hands in delight while Gwen rolled her eyes dramatically. "Great, so now I'm going to have to cover for both of you while you dillydally with those nudists."

"They're not nudists," Trudy said with a frown. "The Postcards are naughty, but not pornography. It was so much fun last year. Oh, please say you'll do it, Landry! You'll be amazing. I heard they were going to use a theme of the Olympics this year. I'd love to see you pose as one of the famous statues, wearing only a wreath of laurel leaves... and a nude thong."

"Sign me up," Landry exclaimed, more than ready to shed his clothes for the good of the order. Hell, he'd done a production of *Hair* in college. He could certainly go full monty in the name of Dickens.

"Great! You'll have to come to the workshops next weekend. I'm not sure you were planning to...."

Landry shrugged. "As long as Gwen doesn't mind bossing our handymen around."

Gwen's eyes flared. "I will hate no such thing! Tell me, is that sex-on-a-stick Terrence coming? He's way too hot for his own good."

Landry smiled. Terrence and his brother, Sam, were two of Landry's college buddies. They'd been stagehands in the theater program with Landry at Cal State East Bay. They'd gone into business as general contractors, but they were always down to help with stage-craft, and what Landry wanted to put on at Dickens was an entire experience for his patrons. A lovely shop, plenty of personal attention, beverages, and the finest corsets and other garments their hard-earned dollars could buy. Everyone deserved to feel beautiful when dressing up for their favorite occasions.

"Terrence and Sam will be building the booth for us, under your direct supervision. I'll give you the plans, and you'll be the perfect person to crack the whip on those two."

Gwen fanned herself. "Fantastic. Can I order them to work shirtless?"

"You can try." Landry didn't think it would take too much to get

Terrence shirtless. Gwen was a gorgeous lady with dark brown skin and natural hair. She was a trained opera singer with a voice that could slay whole auditoriums, even a cappella, and she was a damn fine seamstress. He'd hired her right after taking over the business, and she made a perfect second-in-command. She had many suitors trying to win her affections.

"Do or do not, there is no try," Trudy said in a Yoda voice. She was an adorable oddball with dyed black hair cut in heavy straight across bangs and pigtails with knee-high socks and minidresses whenever she wasn't in costume. She was a cosplayer extraordinaire, and her talents had been a welcome addition to Landry's shop. If only she could do math. Gwen and Landry took turns overseeing her orders and measurements. She totally understood and encouraged their oversight, fully acknowledging that her math skills left much to be desired.

"Well, then it's settled. How do I get in touch with the director? Should I just email? Text? Carrier pigeon?"

"She's on the directory," Trudy said, pulling out her phone. "We all are." She shoved it in his face. "Dover's number is here as well."

Landry's lip curled into a smile. It was tempting, to be sure. He fired off a quick email to the director of the show, and then he sent a text to Dover.

Should I apologize for last night?

5

October
Dover

"Who is it?"

Darwish leaned over Dover's shoulder as he frowned at his phone. They'd been practicing for three hours for their show the next weekend, and it was definitely time for a water break. It had been a while since they'd gigged, maybe two months this time. The guys in the band were busy with life, especially Darwish, who'd gotten scary news this week. Miranda had started having contractions, and the doctor put her on bedrest to try to keep the bun in the oven for a few more weeks. Her mother was staying with them to be of support, which meant Darwish was free to hang with the guys for the evening, and given his current distracted state, he really needed the break.

"Nunya," Carl said. He was their rhythm guitar player, and he and Darwish riffed on each other constantly.

"Who?" Darwish asked.

"None of ya business, dude. Let the man get some play."

"How do you know he's getting play?" Darwish tucked his pick into the neck of his guitar before setting the instrument aside. His long hair was sticking to his face. He pulled it back in a hair tie and scowled at Carl.

"Yeah," Dover asked. "What makes you assume this is about play?"

Carl shook his head. "Look at you, man. Rubbing at your chin, pulling at your lip. Damn, Dover, you got someone?"

Darwish's living room either got hotter all of a sudden, or Dover's face was flushed: a dead giveaway he had something to hide.

"Aw, shit. Dude!" Carl must have forgotten he was on Dover's side here. "Who is it? What's up?"

"I refuse to answer that question on the grounds I might incriminate myself—"

"Incriminate?" Darwish asked, shocked. "Dover, what have you been up to?"

Dover tapped out *who is this?* before this texting conversation went anywhere near improper. He had a feeling it was Landry, but he wasn't sure.

Was there someone else who accosted you in a restroom last night who needs to apologize?

Dover knew it was useless to fight the smile creeping onto his face, but he also knew he was about to get a world of shit from his best friends. He tried to be hasty with his response.

Not that I recall. And no need to apologize.

Carl whooped and did a little improvisational spanking dance around Darwish's living room.

Darwish stood there gaping at him.

Greg, their drummer, walked in and stopped in the doorway. "What did I miss?"

Carl's dance devolved into a series of pelvic thrusts. "Dover's gonna get some, Dover's gonna get some."

"Wow," Dover said. "How old are we?"

"Who is it? Do I know him?" Darwish asked.

Dover knew it was pointless to hide the truth. Miranda had probably told him—

"Holy shit! Landry? He texted you?"

Dover turned his back as his phone buzzed again, and both Darwish and Carl looked over his shoulder.

"He accosted you in the bathroom?" Carl asked. "Oh, shit. Dude, we need details."

"He was drunk. It didn't mean anything."

"Uh, I've been around a lot of drunk dudes, and none of them kissed me in the can. That's some bold moves."

"But *Landry*?" Darwish asked. "I thought you guys were like rivals or something. Miranda said you had a stick up your ass about him. What's the deal? Wait, were you drunk too? You must have been. You don't usually kiss random dudes. Or dudes you have beef with."

"I don't have beef with him. He's just... different. We have nothing in common."

"Well it's not like you have to have anything in common to kiss someone in a public restroom. You think too much, Dover."

He wished it was that easy, but Landry didn't mean anything by it. He couldn't have. He—

Okay, I'm sorry it was in the restroom, but I'm not sorry I kissed you. I want to see you. I think you want to see me too, at least I hope so. Can we make this happen?

"Invite him to the gig," Carl said. "I gotta see this dude."

"He's not into our music. He'd probably hate it. He's more into, like, Broadway. Show tunes. Look, this is a bad idea—"

Carl grabbed his phone while Darwish held Dover in place by the arms.

"Dover. Listen to me. You've been alone for a long time. Don't you get tired of being alone?"

"Carl! No, Darwish. I happen to like being alone."

It was mostly true. He didn't mind being alone. But something about Landry made him want to venture out of his comfort zone a bit. Which had him unsettled. What could there be to gain by spending time with the guy who loved being center of attention, who was hotter than the sun, and who was considerably younger than him?

What could it hurt?

"I told him you wanted him to come to the show."

"You didn't. Carl!"

"I didn't. But you should invite him."

Dover took a deep breath and responded.

I have a gig next Saturday and then I'll be busy with work and fair. I'll be at the build next weekend.

He didn't want to seem like a dick, but he didn't have the bandwidth to add anything else to his plate right now. Everything was on course, and with this being the busiest season for him, he couldn't afford to get derailed, no matter how much he'd been thinking about that kiss.

Is this gig open to the public? I think I'm ready to broaden my musical horizons.

Dover felt a jolt of emotion go through him. Fear? Lust? Excitement? It seemed cliché and a little immature to hope the guy he liked would come see his band. He hadn't been that guy when he was younger, so why the hell would he start now?

Because *Landry*.

Before he could think any more about it, he sent Landry the details, assured him he didn't need to bother if he was busy, and put his phone away so he wouldn't be tempted to check it again. "Are we going to finish going through the set or what? Let's do this."

After two more sweaty hours of practice in Darwish's living room, they called it quits. Dover loaded up his gear into his truck, which was thankfully back from the shop, and drove home. He tossed his keys and wallet on the table in his town house and was just about to strip and shower when his phone buzzed in his back pocket. He'd gotten more texts tonight than probably in the last month.

I can hardly wait.

Yeah, Dover was going to need a cold shower.

6

November
Landry

LANDRY STRUGGLED to pay attention to what seemed like way too many instructions for a role in the Naughty French Postcards show that simply required him to be mostly nude and posed like a Grecian Olympian, but the director, Susan, was particular about her models and costuming. He'd posed until his muscles strained and then posed some more, wondering just why the hell he'd needed to complicate any more of his life right at this moment, and thinking the whole time about how tonight might go.

He was going to watch Dover play guitar in his prog rock cover band, whatever that meant.

He was going to watch Dover play guitar.

He couldn't wait.

"Thanks, guys!" Susan shouted, letting them know rehearsal was over. "See you tomorrow."

Landry attempted to dash out, grabbing Trudy by the arm as he was giving her a ride.

"What's your hurry?" Trudy said as she trotted to keep up with Landry.

"Dover has a gig tonight, and he sort of invited me. I might have invited myself, but we're going to pretend he asked me."

Trudy snorted. "Fair enough. Wait! He's in a band? What kind of band?"

"I guess it's prog rock? I don't know, something like Rush, I think."

"OMG, I love Rush! Let me come with you. That way I can drive your car back when he invites you home with him," she chuckled, pulling out her phone.

"Wait, what? What are you doing?"

"Gwen wanted us to hang out tonight, so I'm telling her to meet us."

"No, no, no don't do that, Trudy—"

"Awesome! She said Terrence and Sam are coming with. She promised them beers after their hard work today."

Landry sighed. He didn't want to be rude, but he'd wanted to get Dover alone, and Dover never seemed excited about Landry's crowd.

"Okay, are you ready?"

Landry took one look at Trudy, all excited to go out on the town with her best friend, and he crumpled. "Ready as I'll ever be."

DOVER'S DIRECTIONS had been that the bar was called the Dirty Bird Lounge, and that it was on B Street in Hayward. After searching for nearby parking, he and Trudy met up with Gwen, Terrence, and Sam outside the bar. They'd been there for a bit and were enjoying a nice coffee huddled together in the evening chill.

"Are you ready to watch your man?" Gwen asked him quietly. At least his girls weren't broadcasting to the world that they were here to watch Landry's latest crush.

"I think I need a drink or five."

Several drinks later, Terrence had them all in stitches talking about Gwen's management skills.

"How was I supposed to know? It ain't like I got a degree in engineering. I bet you couldn't sew your way out of a paper bag, so hush, now."

"I'm just teasing, G. You made a great boss today. You can boss me around anytime."

Gwen fanning herself had the group in hysterics.

And then they heard guitars.

Landry swung around and nearly spilled his drink when he got a look at the man who'd tormented him for weeks now.

Dover's long hair was down around his shoulders, falling past the middle of his back. Long, dark brown curls framed his intense face, and *mercy*, he'd grown a soul patch. Landry's legs went weak. He wished they were alone already. Just seeing the guy in faded jeans and a tight long-sleeved black T-shirt, with his guitar slung low, had Landry keyed up.

Trudy led them over to a table closer to the stage, practically dragging Landry, who was more focused on Dover than where he was going. He tripped over a couple of chairs before they got to the table.

And Dover saw him.

He wanted to believe he'd seen Dover's eyes light up for a brief moment, but then all he saw was a scowl as the band kicked into their first song.

Landry was completely enraptured by the music, but mostly by watching Dover play and interact with his friends. He actually smiled freely. He didn't sing; that was left to Miranda's husband, Darwish, and the drummer, whom they introduced as Greg, but the guitar parts on these particular songs sounded quite intricate and complicated. Dover never seemed to miss a beat, making it look easy.

After playing for about an hour, Darwish announced they were taking a break. Landry hoped he'd get to talk to Dover, at least say hello, but Dover never appeared. Landry kept an eye out for him, but his group was quite rowdy. Sam had bought at least two rounds of shots, which Landry had declined. He didn't want alcohol to negatively impact his interaction with Dover tonight. Plus, he was driving, although Trudy had been nursing a beer all night and would be fine to drive if need be.

Fifteen minutes later the band took the stage once more and launched into their next set. Landry recognized a couple of the songs they played as more radio-friendly Rush and Yes songs. The "Round-about" he knew from a current slate of memes on the internet that he'd look at whenever he needed to de-stress. The other song was "Subdivisions," one he'd heard as a young man, and he could relate to the message of conform or be cast out. Young Landry had refused to do either and managed to be both a theater enthusiast and one of the popular kids in his high school.

Dover lost himself to the rhythm, his hair sometimes obscuring his face as his fingers flew effortlessly up and down the neck of the guitar. Landry rested his chin in his hand and sighed. The man was so talented and so unassuming. He'd probably be satisfied to stay in the shadows as long as he got to perform his music and create his art.

Landry could respect that. Landry sought admiration for his creations. He drew satisfaction and fulfillment from the joy his garments brought to other people, and he loved performing, whether it was in a play, in his shop, or his latest role in the Naughty French Postcards show. He loved attention—he'd been given plenty as a child —but he was driven to make people happy through his performances. Perhaps someday he'd need to analyze just what he was lacking that had him craving that fulfillment, but tonight, he was more intrigued by why Dover didn't seem to need it.

Another hour passed before the band took yet another break, and this time Landry was determined to talk to Dover. He left the table without announcing his intention, dissuading his peanut gallery from giving their opinions. Dover stood on the side of the stage, drinking a glass of water and talking to Darwish.

"Hey," Landry said when he approached.

Darwish turned on him with wide eyes but accepted his handshake.

"How's Miranda?" Landry asked. He'd texted her after hearing she was on bedrest and asked if there was anything he could do. She'd simply said to keep an eye on Dover. He'd keep both eyes and whatever else Dover would allow at this point.

"Good. She's got her mom and Netflix. If she wasn't worried about the baby, she'd be delighted. Her last doctor's visit went well, so she's to do more of the same. Excuse me, will you?"

Darwish walked off toward the bar, and he was finally alone with Dover.

"You guys sound great. Thank you for inviting me."

Dover shrugged and took another drink of his water, emptying the glass.

"How long have you guys been playing together?"

Dover gazed off in the direction Darwish was headed. "Since college. It's hard to find many people who love what we love, so we stick together." He shook the ice around in his glass, watching it move.

"It's obvious you guys are comfortable together. It's fun watching you."

"Thanks, I think."

And then awkward silence set in. What had he done this time? It seemed like they'd had a breakthrough, and now Dover seemed irritated once again.

"Hey, Dover? Am I keeping you?" He had to ask. Dover's body faced away from his, and he looked everywhere but at Landry.

"You brought quite a group."

Landry looked to his friends, who were trying unsuccessfully not to stare.

"Yeah. I told Trudy where I was coming, and the next thing you know, the whole gang is here."

Dover nodded and set his glass down. "Well, don't let me keep you."

"I came to see *you*." He stepped a little closer but was careful not to crowd the man. "Was I wrong to come?"

"It depends on why you came."

"I wanted to see you."

Dover looked as though he might loosen up, and then one of Landry's friends, maybe Sam, made an obnoxious noise, and Dover closed up right in front of him.

"Look, you seem to be comfortable with a big group of people. Maybe this was a mistake."

"It just sort of happened. I didn't think it would be a problem. It's a bar, right? You have a pretty big crowd."

It was true; there were at least fifty or sixty other people in the bar to see the show. *Why is he so upset?*

"Landry, I can't compete with your entourage, and I don't want to. But you're you, and I wouldn't want that to change."

Landry felt the opportunity to get to know this man slipping away fast. They stared at each other, longing so evident in Dover's gaze, but then he shut it off.

"I gotta get ready for the last set."

For a split second, Landry saw the hurt and disappointment Dover tried hard to cover up. Perhaps it was his own issues, but Landry couldn't help but feel he'd made a grave mistake tonight. Apparently, Dover had hoped to be alone with him, which was exactly what Landry wanted too.

"Dover?"

He turned to face Landry, but he was already walking away.

"I'm sorry," Landry said, frustrated. "I only wanted to see you again."

Dover pursed his lips and exhaled through his nose, shook his head slightly, and went to the bar. Landry's heart sank as he saw him get another glass of water and then walk back to the stage, purposely avoiding Landry.

Landry'd had enough. He was exhausted physically from the rehearsals, and now emotionally wrecked.

How much more straightforward could he be with this guy? If Dover couldn't see that he genuinely wanted to spend time with him, perhaps this idea of the two of them getting together and seeing whether their attraction could be something more was wishful thinking. They were very different. Maybe too different.

"Trudy, I'm going home. Do you want a ride?"

Trudy looked from Landry, to Dover onstage, to Landry, to Gwen, and then she gave him a pitying glance. "Do you want me to come with you?"

He smiled and shook his head. "I'll see you at workshops tomorrow."

She kissed his cheek, and he said goodbye to the rest of his now-stunned friends. He rushed out the door before having to answer any more questions.

Time to focus on Dickens. He had some more garments he wanted to finish this week, and opening weekend was fast approaching. Trying to navigate the emotions of Dover was an endeavor he did not have energy for any longer.

7

November
Dover

HE'D LOOKED FORWARD to the gig all week. Good times with his best friends making music, and perhaps a little one-on-one time with one confounding blond who had him tied up in knots. But then Landry decided to bring his entourage to the show, and they proceeded to stare at the two of them, giggling like it was a high school dance. Nope. Not what he had in mind.

He may have been short with Landry, but it was just as well. He had plenty of people around him. Why would Landry possibly be bothering with an ancient curmudgeon like Dover?

"Hey, give me a hand with this, would you?" Greg was attempting to load the drum kit carefully into his beat-up—he referred to it as vintage—minivan and the lift gate didn't want to stay up. Dover held it while Greg hoisted his toms up. "Thanks, man. Let me grab Carl's amp."

Dover stood there holding the gate while Greg struggled with the heavy Marshall amp. He almost had it up when it started to slip from his hand. Dover reached for it, losing his grip on the lift gate, which came crashing down on both of them. He shouted for Greg to watch out and ducked to avoid getting brained with the damn thing. Greg reached for the lift gate and let go of the amp. Dover caught the amp a second before it hit the ground, and something in his right hip gave out. Stabbing pain shot through his lower back, and he crumpled to the ground, setting the amp down gently as he fell.

"Dude! Nice save." Carl and Darwish came trotting over with their guitar cases.

"You all right?" Darwish asked.

Dover had to concentrate on not vomiting. He took breaths to steady himself, but when he tried to shift his weight in order to stand, the knife dug a little deeper, and he had to remain seated on the ground.

"Hey, are you hurt?"

He didn't have the composure to answer.

"Shit," Carl said. "This is bad."

BAD WAS AN UNDERSTATEMENT. Although his X-rays and an MRI showed nothing serious like a disk injury, he had a bad sprain, and the doctor at the ER wrote him off work for at least a week with ample muscle relaxers and pain medicine.

"If you've never had a back injury before, you're in for a rough time of it. Stay flat on your back as much as you can. Ice and heat, you can alternate. Arnica gel might work if you have someone to put it on for you. Other than that, rest. That's all I can tell you. It's going to suck."

"Thanks. I think."

AND, BOY, did it suck. Darwish brought him food daily, mostly at Miranda's insistence, and his dad and Hillary came up to stay with him. They'd planned to come for the opening weekend of fair anyway, so they came a few days early. Dover only had the booth half-built, so his dad went over to finish and visit with his old friends, leaving Hillary to care for Dover and his gloomy self.

He'd hoped to get more inventory done for the fair, but he literally could do nothing but lie in bed and listen to audiobooks and Volume on SiriusXM. And think.

How he'd been a dick to Landry. Again.

How he needed Dickens to be successful so he could buy a new lathe, and this wasn't helping.

How he really wished he hadn't been awful to the man he couldn't stop thinking about. He was certain this time the guy would leave him alone, and for some reason, despite thinking that's what he wanted, he felt a loss. Which was weird. It wasn't like he had him in the first place. One kiss did not a relationship make.

"That frown is so intense, I almost wondered whether I should disturb you, but you need to eat and take more drugs."

He tried to smile at Hillary, but then he rolled over so he could push himself up on the side of his bed and was reminded of his injury. "You're not disturbing me. My own stupidity is disturbing me."

"Ah," she said, sitting on the edge of the bed with the tray, ready to hand it to him when he was settled. "What did you do, or not do, this time?"

He scoffed. "You act like I am stupidity often."

She chuckled and smiled at his slurred speech. He'd been blessed with a fantastic stepmother who made his father happy when he'd worried he'd never see his father smile again.

"You are your father's son." She patted his knee and waited patiently as he got settled into the wing-back chair in his room so he could eat.

"True. No, I... I think I hurt someone's feelings. I didn't mean to, but—"

"But you're you, and you probably told him how you really felt. Yeah, not everyone can take that."

"Does that make it right?"

"Would you rather do something or be someone you're not in order to please others?"

He stirred his spoon around in the soup she'd made and exhaled. "No, of course not. But do I just leave well enough alone? Do I apologize and ask to be friends?"

"Are either of those what you want?"

Dover didn't have to think too hard this time. He knew what he wanted. Another chance with Landry, which would have to wait until he was better. Unfortunately.

"No." He wanted more.

AFTER A WEEK, Dover saw his primary care physician and was told he needed another week of rest. He had the leave at work, that was no problem, but Dickens started next weekend, and his booth wasn't quite ready. He went over with his father, but he was in too much pain to do anything other than look around.

"How the heck am I supposed to work, Dad?"

"You're going to let your old man cover for you, son. Let me take this weekend. You need the rest. Just show me what's what, and we'll make it work."

He hated admitting defeat. He refused to accept it would be for longer than the first weekend. Dover gazed across the aisle to the booth he'd wanted for himself and knew instantly that the organizers of the event had made the right choice.

Landry had created a wonderland for his customers. There were settees for his guests to lounge upon while waiting for their measurements to be taken, or for their family members to be comfortable with a glass of wine or champagne while they took their turn in the windows. Dover smiled to himself. Landry was a genius, and Dover knew the purveyor of fine period garments would make a killing.

So Dover went home to recuperate and put his control-freak tendencies aside as his father handled his business for him.

8

*O*pening weekend
Landry

"WHO'S THE guy over in Dover's booth?"

It was opening morning of Dickens Fair, and the crowds had just been let in after the promenade. The exhibition barns of the Cow Palace were decorated to the hilt with holiday festivity, and the sounds of Christmas carols echoed through the bays. Landry already had a full booth, and he'd conned Sam and Trudy to take their turns in the windows for the first session. They really made a lovely pair. Perhaps life would imitate art for his friends.

"I don't know," he answered Terrence, who'd also volunteered to work the first weekend and help them host their customers. "I'm guessing he brought someone else since Miranda can't work."

Landry had been trying all morning not to search for Dover, but two weeks hadn't been enough time to erase his desire for him. The night of Dover's gig hadn't gone at all as he'd hoped, and Dover had walked away from him, but he still held out hope something, anything, might happen to change Dover's mind. He'd even stupidly hoped maybe Dover would call or text him, but he should have known better.

"That's his father," Gwen said as she passed by. "Dover hurt his back."

Landry swung around and dropped the pair of pantalettes he needed to bring to a guest in the dressing area.

"What did you say?"

Gwen raised an eyebrow and nodded. "The night of the gig. After you left. I heard from Jennifer over in the Family Parlor that Dover's father was taking over until he's able to work. Sounds like it was pretty bad."

Landry turned to gaze across the aisle and, actually, now that he was looking, he did see there was a family resemblance. Unlike Dover, however, his father smiled quite a bit. He had the same nose and jawline and was a little bit taller than Dover.

"Maybe you should go talk to him?" Gwen stood at his side and nudged him. "We've got things under control here."

He looked down at her with a sad smile. "And say what? 'Hello, Mr. Billings, you don't know me, but I'm completely enamored of your son. He has told me in so many ways to leave him alone, and yet I can't get the hint and move on. Would you put in a good word for me?' Because we both know that's the truth. Dover doesn't want anything to do with me, and yet I can't walk away. I have problems."

Gwen looked at him and gave him one more gentle nudge in the direction of Dover's booth before walking away.

He took a deep breath and crossed the aisle.

"Hello! Welcome to Cliffs of Dover Designs. In the market for a new writing apparatus? Perhaps a glass for reading the fine print on personal documents and contracts."

How adorable. Mr. Billings was quite the thespian; his British accent was spot-on.

"Mr. Billings? I'm Landry Malcolm." He stuck out his hand, and the older man shook it with vigor and a huge smile.

"Derrick, please." Dover's father gave him a once-over and his smile shifted. "Ah. You're the tailor. Your garments are quite dashing." He dropped the accent and leaned in a little, still holding on to his hand. "My son speaks highly of you." He winked as he let go.

Landry was nervous all of a sudden. His hands were so clammy, he inauspiciously wiped them on his trousers. "How is Dover? I heard he was injured?"

Derrick whistled through his teeth and glanced at a few passersby. "He's better than he was, but he's still in a lot of pain, and stubborn to boot. He's not happy to be missing opening weekend. I don't know whether to take that as he doesn't trust me fully to run things or if he's merely sorry he can't watch your shop across the aisle."

Landry wasn't prepared for that last comment. He smoothed his hair back. "He... he mentioned me? Really? I'm surprised. Our last encounter was less than positive."

Derrick rolled his eyes. "My son. So serious. He talked to my wife a bit, but I know my son. Look, you didn't hear it from me, because I really do try not to meddle in his affairs too much, but Dover is... sensitive. He hates the spotlight, even if he was born for it, if you ask me. He's so damned talented. Anyway, when it comes to matters of the heart, he's always shied away from getting involved seriously with anyone. He's had a lot of suitors pass through, but he manages to chase most of them away." He winked at Landry and leaned in to whisper, "Don't be easily deterred."

And with that, he was back to the actor, greeting new customers. He gave Landry a sly smile before turning his attention to their purchases.

Landry took a look around. Dover's crafts were works of art. It was obvious he put his heart and soul into each and every piece he created. The pens were lovely, just the right shape and weight. He'd even made more of his speaker boxes out of lovely wood with various stains. He ran a finger across one in particular that spoke to him. It had a deep reddish stain and had a heart burned into the top. The speakers were on the sides, so from the top it looked like a jewelry box or a place for keepsakes. The wood was so smooth, it seemed too perfectly made to have been crafted by hand. There was a small signature in the bottom corner, and Landry smiled. So unassuming. He took it over to Derrick and paid for it. How could he not? It was perfect.

Dover might try to stay out of the spotlight, but Landry saw him for the talented man he was. He wanted to give him something that would let him know Landry saw him, that he was special and deserving of praise. And given his current situation, Landry had the perfect idea. As soon as the weekend came to a close, he'd get to work on the perfect way to express to Dover that he saw him, and that he liked what he saw.

9

D *over*

HE HADN'T BEEN EXPECTING any deliveries this week, so when the FedEx guy knocked, quite loudly, at 8:00 a.m. on Friday morning, he'd been surprised.

"This one's heavy. Shall I just put it inside for you?"

Dover held the door open farther, and the guy hefted the box and placed it on the floor near the door.

"Thank you," Dover said, frowning. The box was addressed to him, from his father.

"Dad?"

Derrick Billings came out of the kitchen in only pajama pants, with a cup of coffee. "Oh good! It arrived."

Dover didn't trust his peppy attitude.

"What did you do?"

"Replaced your lathe," Derrick said. "You can't very well be without one."

Dover growled. "Dad, I was going to buy one after the season was over. You didn't need to do this."

"Consider it a Christmas gift, son. You need it to stay in business."

"But, Dad, I don't want you cutting into your savings for me."

"I didn't! I've been working."

Dover's eyes bugged out. "What? Why? I thought you told me you guys were in good shape to retire down there." His father was young yet, only sixty-two, but still. "Dad, if you needed money—"

"Please. Son. When have you known me to sit still? I got a sweet gig teaching part-time at the community college down there. One class a semester, and it doesn't interfere with my retirement. But even without the extra money, I could still afford to buy my son a new lathe for his business. Now shut up and give me a hug."

Dover wrinkled his nose. "Maybe when you put a shirt on."

His dad was not to be deterred. He crossed the living room dramatically, and Dover cringed. "Dad, remember. I'm injured."

Derrick hugged him and laughed heartily. "That young tailor Landry came by to see about you."

There was a second knock at the door. Dover looked out the window and saw a UPS driver walking away.

"What the heck is going on?" He opened the door and started to bend to pick up the package, and he sucked in a breath.

"Ah. Why don't you let me handle that, old man?"

"Funny guy," he sneered at his father and lowered himself carefully onto the couch.

"It's for you. Open it."

"What did you do now?"

His father chuckled and shook his head. "Not me. Not this time."

The return address was Oakland, but Dover didn't recognize it. He used one of the letter openers he'd made at the very beginning of his artistic journey. He'd kept it because he'd messed up with the handle a little, and it wasn't perfect, but it stood the test of time. He cut through the tape and marveled at how light the box was. Inside was a thick covering of tissue paper. He lifted out an envelope with an old-fashioned wax seal on it with the initial M.

. . .

DOVER,

I am terribly sorry about your injury. Word travels quickly at fair, I'm sure you're familiar with how things work. I wanted to do... something. I made this garment for you, you can wear it or not, but I wanted to explain some of the special features. It is built specially to support the lower back without looking like a bulky back brace. I've also created pockets on the inside to place heat or ice packs to help with your recovery. The lining on the inside is also removable and machine washable in case you want to use any sort of pain-relieving liniments. I used my best judgment to size it. Regrettably I wasn't able to get your exact measurements, but you can adjust it to fit comfortably and I can alter it if necessary... and if you decide it is useful. Consider it a peace offering. Here's to your speedy recovery. You are missed at Dickens by all.

Warmest Regards,

Landry Malcolm

DOVER WAS SPEECHLESS.

After everything that had happened, after he'd done everything in his power to push Landry away, he'd gone above and beyond to make something special for him. *Consider it a peace offering.* If anyone should be offering peace, it was Dover.

A sticker with the same print as Landry's seal held the tissue together in the middle. He carefully opened it and gasped at what he found inside.

"What is it, son?"

Dover carefully lifted the corset from the tissue paper. It was an underbust-styled corset with a masculine form and was made from a deep maroon spot broche fabric with silver loops and pins as well as silver antique buttons on the front. It was absolutely breathtaking: a garment so stylish Dover would never have considered wearing something like it before, but now? With the back injury, he was tempted to see if the garment would provide him some relief. He knew many actors over the years who'd sworn by the comfort and support afforded by a little shaping, and he'd always laughed it off before, choosing to wear his modest linen dress shirt and vest with slacks. But this garment would be best worn with trousers and perhaps a cream silk shirt.

Before he got too carried away with whether he would actually wear the thing, he opened it up and, sure enough, within the panels of the corset, between the boning, were slots in the fabric where he could indeed place hot or cold packs. He kept charcoal packs for his hands during Dickens. The back barns were freezing cold for most of the run of the show, and his hands were somewhat arthritic from years of crafting and playing guitar. The heat packs helped to keep him comfortable during the long days of the fair. They would definitely help him get through a day of work.

"That's quite a handsome corset. I never needed to wear one myself, of course. Always kept a trim figure." Derrick stretched his arms out and then ran his hands over his slender physique. Dover snorted. They were built nearly exactly the same, though his father had a couple of inches on him.

"I can't believe he made this for me," Dover breathed, so touched by the gesture. "I was pretty awful to him. Why would he do this?"

Derrick sipped his coffee. "He seems quite smitten with you."

"Derrick." Hillary had joined them and gave Derrick a disapproving headshake. "Don't stir the pot."

A flicker of hope wavered in Dover's heart. Could he possibly receive that second chance? Did this gift mean Landry might—

"You *are* going to work this weekend, are you not?" his father asked him.

"If you're there to help me, yes. I'm not sure how much I can do, and while I'm on these drugs, it might not be the best time for me to be running a business without oversight."

Derrick patted him on the shoulder. "Of course. I'm here for you, son. Now, why don't you model this for us."

With a little help, Dover was fastened into the corset and immediately felt an improvement in his pain level. He studied himself in the mirror, liking the way the corset seemed made for him. He especially liked the buttons. They looked handmade.

"A chip off the old block," Derrick said as he stood behind him in the mirror. "Maybe I'll have to have the young man make one for me. Can't let you have all the fun." He turned and yelled, "Hey, Hillary. Think I should get one of these?"

Hillary stuck her head in Dover's room and pressed a hand to her chest. "Sure. But maybe not the nipple piercings."

Dover laughed and ran a self-conscious hand over his chest.

Derrick took a look and winced. "Yeah, I don't think so. I still can't believe you got that done. Tattoos I get, but the piercings...?"

Dover shrugged. "They're not for everyone." He turned back to look at Landry's handiwork. It must have taken him hours to make something so incredible. Dover began formulating a plan. He wanted to create a peace offering of his own for the man who was patient enough to put up with him. Now that his father had replaced his lathe, he knew just what to make for Landry. He'd get on it this afternoon. Now that he had the extra support, his back should be able to handle a couple hours of work.

10

S econd weekend of December
    Landry

LANDRY WAS DETAINED by a very touchy-feely woman who was overly excited about her new corset design. He was late to call for the Post-cards show and wondered for the umpteenth time why he'd signed on for the additional commitment when the shop was taking up all his energy. The show *was* fun; he'd ended up being needed to perform rather than understudy, and that was all fine, but he felt like he was running on fumes.

What kept him going, however, was that Dover was back... and he was wearing the corset.

Landry's tongue had fallen out of his mouth like a cartoon char-acter when he'd caught his first glimpse, and he'd been distracted ever since. Dover wore the corset paired with charcoal trousers and a new cream shirt. He'd obviously taken care with his appearance, and Landry was nearly panting. The stubborn man was so damn sexy, and he didn't even seem to be aware.

"Hurry up! Your pose is coming up," Trudy scolded. She helped him out of his clothes and placed the laurel wreath on his head. Directly after this evening's show, they were doing an after-hours show for the fair folk, since the vendors couldn't exactly all walk away from their booths and come watch.

"You got your thong on?"

"Yes. I forgot it last week and had to run back, so I threw it on this morning. It's been riding up all day, thank you very much."

Trudy giggled. "Welcome to the neighborhood." She patted him down with powder to give him the alabaster sheen of the statue he was imitating.

"Oh, pipe down. All right. Everything in place? Ready to go?"

She gave him a once-over and touched up a few spots. "Looks good. Nothing hanging out."

He rolled his eyes. "Wonderful."

He hurried to his spot and was getting into place when the screen was illuminated to show his nearly naked form in the famous pose of the discus thrower. The audience cheered loudly and applauded, a few familiar voices making catcalls. He fought the urge to laugh, holding his pose for several long moments while the actors made their jokes, and then it was time for the next actor to take their spot.

Back in the dressing area, he threw on a robe to ward off the chill before he went and did his pose again for the next show. Trudy did her part and then joined him, laying out some snacks she'd brought for them.

"Peanut butter and jelly never tasted so good," he said, moaning. He hadn't eaten since breakfast as the shop was too busy in the middle of the day for him to sneak off.

"You're welcome. It was all I had to throw together."

"And it hit the spot perfectly."

They went out for their bow and then returned backstage as they waited for the Victorian London to clear out of fairgoers. Then it was time for the bawdy songs, which he knew by heart by now. They came out at the most ridiculous times. He caught himself singing one while making a deposit at the bank the past week, and the teller gave him the strangest look.

He allowed himself to sit down and knew it was a mistake when Trudy shook him awake what felt like five minutes later.

"You fell asleep! It's almost your turn."

Shit. He jumped around and slapped at his face to try to wake up. He was going to sleep like a rock tonight.

"You're on."

He hurried out to his spot, hit the pose... and got a cramp in his calf. *Holy God in Heaven!* He held still and screamed internally, never losing his pose, but when the lights went out, he hobbled back to the dressing room and fell into the chair, rubbing frantically at the cramp.

"Are you all right?"

Dover appeared in the doorway, a worried look on his face.

"Cramp. Ow."

Dover hurried over, pulled up a stool, and lowered himself carefully onto it, wincing a bit as he sat.

"Don't. You're hurt."

"Shut up. Here, give me your leg."

Landry did as he was told and placed his right foot on Dover's thigh, letting out a string of curses as he moved.

Dover pulled a package out of his pocket and ripped it open. "I have one more of these. The heat should help." He shook the charcoal packet used to warm the hands and then pressed it against Landry's calf.

"Ohhhhmygodddd, thank you. That hurt like the dickens."

Dover grinned a little at Landry's joke, and then he began massaging the muscle, his strong hands getting right to the knot.

Landry moaned and slid down in the cushioned chair, his eyes rolling back in his head. "Yesss, that's so much better. God, you're good at that. Thank you."

"No problem." He continued to knead Landry's calf, moving away from the area of the cramp. "It's the least I could do." Dover glanced down at the corset he wore so well and smiled shyly. "The corset is wonderful."

"It looks amazing on you. I'd hoped I got the size right."

"This is the nicest thing anyone's ever made for me," Dover said in a quiet voice. "Really. Thank you. I wouldn't have been able to work all day if I hadn't had it. I appreciate that you took the time to make something so beautiful."

Landry opened one eye and smiled, enjoying the feel of Dover's hands and the sight of him between his thighs. His very naked thighs. Landry was dressed only in the thong he'd worn for his pose in the Postcards performance and therefore continued to put on quite a show. He gasped when Dover hit a particularly sensitive spot, and Dover grunted a little, a sound like he'd made when they kissed... so long ago.

"I knew when I came to see the show tonight that I was seeing the Postcards—I've seen it before—but I wasn't prepared to see this much of you."

Dover's eyes traveled over Landry's body. Suddenly it wasn't cold anymore in the back barns of the Cow Palace, and Landry was no longer tired. He sat up straight and their eyes met. "Did you enjoy the show?"

Dover stopped kneading, his touch becoming more of a caress. "I did. One pose in particular."

Landry slid his foot up Dover's thigh and let it fall toward the floor, his leg now draped over Dover's lap. He rested his forearms on Dover's shoulders and pressed their foreheads together. "Is that so?"

"Mmm-hmm," Dover murmured. He slid his hands up the outside of Landry's thighs to his hips, letting his fingers drift over the elastic of the thong. "I guess I'm quite a fan of the Greek Olympians. I'm suddenly in awe of the discus thrower." He pulled back to gaze into Landry's eyes as if waiting for permission.

"Please kiss me," Landry breathed. "I don't even care if it's just a kiss and nothing more. I can't go a second longer without kissing you again."

Dover chuckled. "Always with the drama."

And he kissed him. And Landry was so damn grateful that he'd asked because it was even better than before when he'd been tipsy and wanton in the men's room. He moaned and wrapped his arms around Dover's neck, pulling him closer and deeper into the kiss.

Dover knelt before him and gripped his waist. He took control of the kiss, licking, sucking, and nipping at Landry's eager lips as though trying his mouth on for size. Landry felt as though Dover was taking his measure, and he allowed himself to fantasize what it would be like to be completely at Dover's mercy.

"Landry, you're late for— Oh!" Trudy covered her mouth and giggled. "Nothing! You're late for nothing. I see nothing." She scurried out of the curtained-off dressing area, getting caught in the drapes on her way out.

"I'm—oops?"

Dover shook his head. "It's fine." He traced Landry's ribs with his thumbs. "I've come to accept that one rarely gets to be alone with Landry Malcolm."

Landry dipped his head to look into Dover's eyes. "And you're okay with that?" He knew Dover's major hang-up had to do with Landry being center of attention. He'd said he didn't want Landry to change, but could he really accept it? "My friends are my friends. I can't help that. But I can promise that if we go back to my house right now, no one will interrupt us."

11

D*ecember*
Dover

D**OVER'S HEART** pounded nearly out of control at the thought of taking Landry home and not worrying about interruptions. He wasn't even upset that Trudy had walked in. At this point, everyone knew there was something between them. He'd gotten comments all day about how wonderful his corset was (everyone), how Landry had been so hopeful that he'd like it and wear it (Trudy and the rest of the cast of the Postcards show), and whether he'd be modeling it in the windows (Gwen and his father). He'd been embarrassed at first, but he recalled how touched he'd been to wear something Landry had made just for him. Then he wore it with pride. A gift like this was something to be treasured, as the gift of Landry's affection was. Part of the reason Landry was always surrounded by people was that he gave so much to everyone. He made people feel special, feel good, so naturally people were drawn to his light.

Dover was drawn to him for all of these reasons and more. Right now, he was drawn in by something much more carnal.

"Your house. No interruptions. I like the sound of that. And as much as I like you basically naked, you probably should put some clothes on, or you'll cramp up again."

"If I have you to work out the knots, I'd practically not even care."

Dover stood carefully, wincing a bit. The corset had certainly helped, but he needed another dose of medication and a flat surface. If that surface happened to have naked Landry next to him, all the better.

THEY BARELY MADE it to the lot without being waylaid, and found they'd parked next to each other. They laughed, and Dover put his arm around Landry.

"I can always give you a ride tomorrow."

"I'm hoping you'll give me a ride tonight *and* tomorrow."

Dover chuckled and pulled him closer and down for another kiss, thinking horizontal was going to be quite a delight. He unlocked the door and opened it for Landry. He took a moment to breathe as he walked around the rear of the truck. His hands were shaking like this was his first prom date or something. He slid inside and blew into his freezing cold hands before starting the engine. Steppenwolf blared over the speakers, and he burst out laughing.

"Who are you and what have you done with my dour Dover?"

Dover backed out of the parking spot with a smile. *His Dover. I like the sound of that.* "Keep listening."

Landry frowned until he heard the chorus. "'Magic Carpet Ride'?"

They both laughed as they sped down Highway 101 toward Landry's house and a night of no interruptions.

12

L *andry*

THEY MADE it to Landry's in record time as it began to rain. They pulled up to his tiny early twentieth-century bungalow in the San Leandro Hills before ten, the excitement tangible between them the entire ride. Landry unlocked the door and cursed when he recalled he hadn't cleaned up his current project mess, which took up his entire living room. That and the fact that he had a naked Christmas tree waiting until he actually had time to decorate it with the ornaments that were already unwrapped and sitting on the coffee table, ready to go. What a disaster.

"This is where you pretend you are so enamored of me that you don't notice my house is a wreck. Follow me." Landry took his hand and led him quickly through the piles of material, cutting boards, dress forms, and tools, past the miniscule kitchen and the dinky washroom to his slightly roomier master bedroom. When his grandmother decided to move in with his parents in Piedmont, Landry had bought out her mortgage. He'd had so many fond memories of child-hood sewing adventures with her that he'd never let this place go to a stranger. He didn't care much about the size, except when his friends all decided he needed to host gatherings, but then he had a fantastic multilevel patio out back complete with heaters and a sound system. *Music.*

"I'm just going to freshen up. Stereo's over there. Pick something you like. I'll be right out."

He could barely breathe with Dover in his space, he was so excited. After everything that had happened during their year of misunderstandings, to have him in his bedroom? His cheeks hurt from smiling.

Landry stripped and hopped in the shower as he heard the music start. It was sort of heavy rock, but not obnoxious. His tastes did run more typical drama geek—show tunes, EDM, and Barry Manilow of course—but he was looking forward to all Dover had to show him.

The door opened.

Landry peeked over the top of the shower door.

Dover unbuttoned his shirt slowly. "Mind if I join you?"

Landry barked out a laugh. "Mine is not the shower for a good time, but yeah, let me finish up real quick, and then I want to watch you."

Landry was becoming quite fond of the little grin Dover seemed to have found tonight. He'd rarely seen the man smile, so he liked to think it was his special grin, meant only for Landry.

He hurriedly washed the powder and funk from the day off of his body and asked Dover to hand him a towel. He didn't cover himself with it, however. He wanted to drink in all of Dover's reactions.

But he wasn't prepared for what he'd find under Dover's clothing.

A massive black-and-gray medieval dragon wound from his shoulder, under his arm, down his left side to his hip. The other side of his torso had a series of runes and celestial figures tattooed.

And both nipples were pierced with silver rings.

"Dover Billings," he breathed. "You are truly a man of mystery."

Dover stepped out of his trousers, and Landry was treated to the most delicious part of his anatomy yet. If he wielded *that* as well as he did his hands, Landry was in for the ride of his life.

"When presented with such an object of beauty," Landry said with a smirk, "one knows not where to begin its admiration."

Yet another grin. Landry intended to keep that sexy smile on Dover's succulent lips.

Dover pulled his hair up into a messy bun and washed efficiently but not in a rush while Landry leaned against the sink and sighed. "All that is mine to pleasure?"

Dover turned the water off and stood dripping, glistening, semi-erect, and marvelous in the shower stall, his hands at his side. "A towel, please?"

He might have sounded annoyed, but his smirk said otherwise. Landry gazed for one more luscious moment before handing him a towel, which he wrapped around his waist. His next move was to pin Landry against the sink, tonguing his throat.

Landry gasped. "What are we listening to?"

"Baroness. 'Take My Bones Away.'"

"Yes, please. Do."

Dover proceeded to do just that.

13

D*over*

WAKING UP tangled with Landry wasn't at all like the rude shock of an alarm clock or the sunlight shining through the window directly into your eye. Waking up tangled with Landry was like sinking your toes into warm sand, slipping into a hot bubble bath, or curling up on a comfy couch in front of a roaring fire. Landry was all of the creature comforts Dover usually denied himself, all at the same time.

Landry slept all over the bed. At first, Dover had kept to a sliver on the far side of the queen-size bed, letting Landry flail, but then he sort of planted himself in Landry's way and was rewarded with a happy sigh and hours of cuddling. Upon waking, Dover took the opportunity to admire his handsome bedfellow, who was definitely going to have to wear a high-collared dress shirt. Dover was confident he owned something that would work given the breadth of Landry's wardrobe, which was visible at the far end of the bedroom. Landry's walk-in closet was nearly the size of a normal bedroom, and from his vantage point on the bed, Dover could see racks of suits and dress shirts and various and sundry Victorian-era accessories.

"I suppose they'll notice if we don't show up," Landry mumbled, his face adorably smashed into Dover's chest.

"I'd imagine so. Susan, your director, will be devastated to lose her discus thrower."

Landry grunted. "I've got an understudy. He can freeze his balls off and get leg cramps."

"My stars." Dover laughed. "I'd assumed the golden boy was all sunshine and rainbows in the mornings."

Landry opened one brown eye and frowned. "Does my grumpiness earn me more or fewer points?"

Dover ran a hand over Landry's perfect ass. "Definitely more. The Scroogier the better, in my humble opinion."

Landry snorted and rolled onto his back. "You don't have a humble bone in your body, Dover Billings."

"I suppose not. I say what I think and do what I want. Is that a problem?"

"Not at all. Not for me. Helps me know where I stand with you."

Dover pushed up on an elbow. "Were you concerned?"

Landry's smile slipped. "This morning? No. The past year? Yeah. I thought you couldn't stand me. I couldn't figure out what I'd done to offend."

Dover sighed. "I really can be a dick. I'm sorry. It was never you. It was about me."

Landry rolled his eyes. "Wow. That helps. Do go on."

"I'm serious. I was attracted to you and couldn't figure out why. You seemed like someone I would have zero in common with, and you were always surrounded by people showering you with attention. I thought at first that I was annoyed, but then I realized my annoyance was with myself."

"Why, though?"

"Because I wanted to be close to you but didn't feel like stepping out of my comfort zone to actually pursue you."

Landry pushed up and leaned against the headboard. "What changed your mind?"

Dover got to his knees and straddled Landry's lap. "When you kissed me."

And morning breath be damned, he was going to have more of Landry's kisses.

THEY HAD to rush to get dressed, and as Dover slid into his freshly pressed trousers—compliments of Landry—he thought about the gift he'd almost given Landry yesterday and was glad he'd waited.

"Here, let me help you into your corset." Landry insisted on fussing over him, and Dover was surprised to be loving every minute of it. His mind had already skipped to the end of the day—coming back here to be undressed by Landry—but first, he wanted to give something back to the man his heart said was for keeping.

"I want to do the windows today. With you."

Landry froze on the third fastener. "Model. With me. Today? Are you *serious*?"

Landry vibrated with excitement and Dover chuckled. The age difference didn't bother him like he thought it might. He found it adorable that Landry was so easily amused. "I'm serious. You can be the master tailor fitting me for the perfect garment."

Landry ran his hands up Dover's torso and dragged his fingers over Dover's nipple piercings. "And show everyone what you've got under your clothes? I think our patrons might be a little shocked when I lose control and perform enthusiastic fellatio in the booth, but hey, I'm up for it if you are."

Dover barked out a laugh and snaked his hands around Landry's hips, grabbing his ass firmly. "I think it's best to save the fellatio for tonight." He kissed Landry's chin, nibbling not quite gently. "I'm not done discovering all the ways I can make you scream."

Landry shuddered and his knees buckled. "Heaven forbid I keep you from your discoveries."

. . .

THEY WERE LATE, but good old Dad had things running smoothly in his booth and Gwen and Trudy already had customers happily shopping. They agreed Dover would come over in the afternoon.

"If we do it any sooner, I'm going to be tenting my trousers all day."

Dover felt the same, but it was so nice to know Landry was suffering too.

His father gave him a stern glance when he arrived.

"I know you're a little old to be getting grounded, but a text would have made your old man sleep a little easier."

Dover blushed and apologized. "I'm sorry if I kept you from getting a good night's sleep."

Derrick raised an eyebrow at him and then chuckled. "I take it you had a good night?"

Dover could only smile. He'd had a wonderful night that felt like the beginning of something special.

"That's my boy," Derrick said, smacking him a little too hard on the back. "Oh, sorry. How's your back this morning?"

Dover wanted to say he was fabulous because not only did Landry have a much more comfortable bed than he did, he'd also gotten a postcoital massage that did wonders for his healing.

"A little stiff, but I'm feeling much better."

His father saw right through him. "I'll bet."

14

L *andry*

DOVER CAME over to his booth close to three o'clock. The plan was they'd take their turn in the windows, and then Landry would dash off to his performance in the Postcards show, leaving Dover to close up shop; then the two of them would drive their separate cars back to Landry's and pick up where they left off until the last possible moment. Dover had said he was on holiday break from his job with the school district, and Landry had already planned to take the day off to recuperate from the weekend, so they had many hours of bliss ahead of them.

"Are you ready to become the most talked-about event in the history of the Dickens Family Christmas Fair?" Landry whispered in his ear, inhaling Dover's incredible scent.

Dover's eyes darted around at all the people gathered. Trudy had told a few people, which at fair translated to everyone and their brother and cousin showing up outside Landry's booth.

"So we'll do what we rehearsed, yeah?" Dover shoved his hands in his pockets and fidgeted with them.

"Of course. If you don't want to do it, I totally understand."

"No. I said I would. I want to do this for you."

Landry knew how hard that had been for Dover, coming out of his comfort zone. He'd been elated when Dover finally explained his reluctance to get involved. Landry could understand. On the surface Landry knew he projected confidence and a carefree spirit, but it took effort at times to keep up that façade. There were many times when he too felt nervous. Like now. This act they were about to perform for the Dickens crowd was intensely intimate. While Landry was affectionate and had many dear friends, he hadn't had a serious boyfriend in a very long time, and he kept his affairs private. Going public with Dover was an intentional step for both of them, for different reasons.

"Let's do this." Dover kissed his cheek and stepped past him into the small booth. He stood with his back to the opening and unbuttoned his shirt. Gasps and squeals sounded outside the window, and Landry could imagine the picture Dover made with his long hair flowing, his tattoos on display, his proud jaw lifted to give that aristocratic air he was totally unaware he had.

Landry stepped in behind him and slid the shirt from his shoulders as he stood perfectly still. Dover raised his arms to the side in a T position, and Landry produced a tape measure, stepping close to wind it around his waist. Being this close to him made Landry's heart pound so loud, he was sure the audience could hear it.

"Your hands are freezing," Dover whispered, and Landry cracked a smile, attempting to hide his face.

"We're not supposed to talk, silly."

They held that pose for a few more beats, and then Dover placed a hand on Landry's and turned to face him.

"I have something for you," he whispered.

He pulled something out of his pocket that was wrapped in a maroon pouch made of suede. Dover cradled it in trembling hands. All of this was done incrementally, their attempt to keep the show authentic. Dover looked up and locked eyes with Landry.

"A peace offering. Happy Christmas."

He slowly moved his hands forward and presented the pouch to Landry.

"What is it?"

Dover gave him his special smile. "I made this for you. Open it."

Landry frowned, totally forgetting about the audience and untied the laces that closed the pouch. He pulled back the sides and sucked in a breath.

Inside was a set of sewing implements used to make corsets. A pair of shears, an awl, and an eyelet setting tool, all with handcrafted handles made of deep burgundy polished wood. They were absolutely beautiful.

"How did you...? When did you...?"

"I ordered some of these kits a while ago. Remember my teacher Mrs. Ramirez? This summer? She was asking me if I could make sewing tools for her. I researched what tools you'd need to make something as beautiful as you made for me, and sure enough, I had what I needed. The wood, I thought, complements the color of the corset. I hope they'll be useful."

Landry wiped at a tear and a sob escaped. It was truly the most wonderful thing anyone had ever done for him, and here he was blubbering in front of everyone.

Dover quickly pulled him in for a hug, and Landry buried his face in Dover's hair.

"I'm sorry, I didn't mean to upset you."

"You didn't. I'm... overwhelmed. These are incredibly thoughtful. I will be so careful with them."

Applause broke out on the other side of the window, and the two men had trouble getting their awkward laughter and tears under control.

"We have to finish," Dover whispered. "The holes in the pouch are there so you can slide it on a belt and wear it, but you don't have to, you know."

"Of course I will! I'm so in love with these, Dover. I will treasure them." He slid the pouch into the inside pocket of his suitcoat and took his time measuring Dover's torso from the sternum down to below his navel while he tried to get his emotions under control.

"I was going to give them to you yesterday. I'm sorry. I probably should have done it a little more privately."

Landry thought back to the perfect night they'd had. "You gave me so much last night," he whispered coyly. "Why not this?"

"Well, I planned on it, but when I found you, you were nearly naked, and then I had other things on my mind."

It was time to end their display. Landry knew they had a mixed audience, and that he'd have to behave, but he couldn't go one more minute. He looped his tape measure around Dover and pulled him closer, planting a kiss on his lips.

They held still with only their lips pressed together while the crowd cheered them on, and that was their reminder not to take the kiss deeper. The passion building between them was akin to a leaky dam ready to burst.

"Happy Christmas, Dover," Landry whispered.

"I can't wait to take you home," Dover replied.

Landry pulled back and found his smile mirrored in Dover's. They turned and took very gentlemanly bows for their audience and then closed the curtains. Landry pulled him in for one more kiss, this time with lots of salacious tongue action, and when Dover made that groan that curled Landry's toes, he knew it was time for them to go.

J*uly*
    Dover

"ARE YOU ALMOST READY?"

It was nearly impossible to get out of the house on time with Landry Malcolm, and they needed to get set up at the TreasureFest. They'd babysat at Darwish and Miranda's the night before for little Adhira and then stayed up for hours talking about babies.

"I'm nearly there, babe," Landry said. "Sorry. Can you grab the coffee and bagels for the ride?"

"Already done."

Dover could only shake his head. He'd been up since five, had showered and made coffee, packed breakfast, hooked Landry's trailer to his truck, and was waiting for Landry to finish getting dressed and whatever else he needed to do to be Landry for the day.

"I'm sorry, I'm sorry," Landry said, finally coming out of the bedroom. He walked straight to Dover and kissed him before walking out the door. "It's really your fault, though. If you hadn't kept me up late—"

"Just get in the truck," Dover said, laughing at his boyfriend's excuses.

The last six months had been both thrilling and insane at the same time. They'd spent all of their free time together, only apart for work and Dover's band practices, which Landry often crashed with his entourage. They'd been doing the monthly art and craft shows on Treasure Island with adjacent booths as well. Landry insisted on stocking Dover's wares in his shop and asked Dover repeatedly to move in with him. Dover finally agreed when school was out for the summer and he could take some time off before he needed to start getting the Chromebooks cleaned up and ready for the next set of students. It had been a month, and Dover had not a single regret.

"I love waking up with you knowing we get to spend the whole day working side by side, then we get to go home and live side by side, and sleep side by side...." Landry ran his hand up Dover's thigh, causing him to swerve a bit.

"It's a little dangerous to be groping the driver," Dover said, not at all upset that Landry loved to touch him all the time. He'd become addicted to Landry's affection and attention. There were times when Landry's penchant for the dramatic got on his nerves, but he'd learned to give himself space by slipping outside to the patio to play his guitar or paint under the covered section of the yard and be fine. In a week or so, Landry was going to help him move his workshop from Darwish's garage into one of the new pair of sheds Landry'd had built on the second level of his backyard. Landry told him he'd been planning to do it anyway, as he needed the storage for his inventory, but Dover insisted on paying for the second one. He'd made plenty of money at Dickens this year, and now that he had shop space to sell his goods during the rest of the year and was renting out his town house, he had additional steady income. He'd thought it would be hard to give up his privacy, but he found he didn't need or want it now that Landry was in his life.

"How's your back this morning?"

The injury had been a recurring issue. Dover would think he was fine, and then he'd work too long or lift something too heavy and he was back on the ice and anti-inflammatories. Landry took care of him when it was bad. He explained that it was the universe's way of telling Dover to take the time to take care of himself.

"Better after you gave me such a nice massage. Thank you, by the way." He brought their linked hands up to kiss Landry's knuckles.

"It was completely my pleasure, love."

Love. Dover had allowed himself to fall in love with Landry and life was good. If someone had asked him last year at this time whether he'd ever find love with an outgoing, life-of-the-party tailor to the stars, he'd have said they were crazy. But that's exactly what he'd done, and he'd been grateful every day since.

"I love you," Dover said, glancing over at Landry. He didn't say it enough; it was weird to say it out loud, but he wanted Landry to know.

"I know you do, and I can't tell you how happy it makes me."

"Mission accomplished."

Treasure Island was packed on this spectacular weekend. Dover loved being on the island that had once been a military installation and that was now mainly used for various vendors, food trucks, and music festivals. Their booths were close to the water, with a phenomenal view of the Bay Bridge.

"Dover! So good to see you again."

Mrs. Ramirez was back. She was so sweet to continue supporting his art after all these years.

He gave her a hug. "How are you, Mrs. Ramirez?"

She squealed. "Your paintings!" She covered her mouth and stepped away from him to get a closer look. "You finally brought them! My God, you've grown so much! These are absolutely stunning."

He'd done a series of paintings based on photos taken at Dickens, of Landry posing in the French Postcards show, of the two of them in the windows together. He'd been so inspired by his newfound love that he'd been driven to paint. Landry had even sat for him, which allowed Dover to worship him with his paintbrush. Those paintings now adorned the walls of the bedroom they shared.

Landry must have seen her come up and decided to join them.

"You remember Mrs. Ramirez?"

Landry took her hand and bowed to kiss the back of it. "Wonderful to see you again."

"It's Ramona, and my goodness, is this you?"

"It is indeed." Landry put his arm around Dover and pulled him in close. "Isn't he fantastic? I'm his biggest fan."

Ramona's eyes widened and darted from the happy couple to the gorgeous paintings. Dover was very proud of them. He thought they were some of his best.

"It's amazing what you can do when you are inspired, isn't that right, Dover?"

Dover gazed up at the man who'd brought good cheer into his Scroogey life. He'd probably smiled more than he ever had in his entire adult life since the night Landry kissed him in a bathroom.

"Absolutely."

ABOUT RO...

Once upon a time... a teacher, tattoo collector, mom, and rock 'n' roll kinda gal opened up a doc and started purging her demons. R.L. MERRILL is still striving to find that perfect balance between real life and happily ever after, and she'll keep writing love stories until she does. Ro writes romance in contemporary, paranormal, and horror settings inspired by love, hope, and rock 'n' roll. Ro also loves connecting with other authors online, at conventions, and as a mentor for the Inclusive Romance Project.

A sucker for underdogs, Ro has adopted a wide variety of pets including cats, dogs, rats, snakes, a chameleon, and some fish. Her love of horror is evident the moment you walk in her door and find yourself surrounded by decorative skulls and quirky artwork from around the world. You can find her lurking on social media where she loves connecting with readers, or else find her educating America's youth, being a mom taxi to two busy kids, in the tattoo chair trying desperately to get that back piece finished, or head-banging at a rock show near her home in the San Francisco Bay Area.

Connect with Ro:

Website: www.rlmerrillauthor.com

Twitter: @rlmerrillauthor
Facebook: www.facebook.com/rlmerrillauthor.com
Instagram: www.instagram.com/rlmerrillauthor
Stay Tuned for more Rock 'n' Romance.

OTHER BOOKS BY R.L. MERRILL

Haunted Series: (Contemporary Romance)

Haunted

Fated

Bated

Minded Series: (Paranormal Spinoff of Haunted Series)

Minded

Blossomed

Father F'in' Christmas

A Peculiar Prom Night

Magic and Mayhem Universe: (Funny Paranormal Romance in the universe created by Robyn Peterman)

Shifted

Ghoul Me Once

Gator Me Twice

Fang Me Three Times

Fangtastic Four

Five Fanger Witch Punch - October 2022

Hollywood Rock 'n' Romance Trilogy: (Contemporary Romance)

Teacher

Teacher: Act Two

Teacher: The Final Act

The Rock Season Series: (Contemporary Romance)

The Rock Season

Road Trip

You Fell First (Previously in Down and Dirty Anthology)

Salty and Sweet (Summer Fair Anthology)

Pinups and Puppies (Originally in Love Is All Vol. 2)

Contemporary Romance by Rochelle Merrill

A Match Made in Spain (Also in Audio!)

Havenhart Academy Series: (Paranormal Romance)

Healer (Also in Audio!)

Connection

Forces of Nature Series: (Gay Contemporary Romance)

Hurricane Reese

Typhoon Toby

Earthquake Ethan (Coming 2023)

Summer of Hush Series: (Gay Contemporary Romance)

Summer of Hush

Brains and Brawn

Book Three (Coming Soon)

Bolder Breed Studios (Queer Romance)

I Want, More – Bolder Breed Studios #1

Love and Pride: Bolder Breed Studios #2

Queer Paranormal Romance

Sundowners

Anthologies:

Thanksgiving Day Parade From Hell (Worst Holiday Ever) (Gay Contemporary Romance

Valentine's Day From Hell (Worst Valentine's Day Ever) (Gay Contemporary Romance)

Salty and Sweet (Summer Fair) (Lesbian Contemporary Romance)

The Fourth Man (The Banes of Lake's Crossing) (Historical Horror Romance)

A Piece of Him (Gone With The Dead) (Horror)

Breaking Bread (Dark Divinations) (Horror)

Exchange (Renewal) (Science Fiction)

Tap-Tap-Tap (Impact) (Horror)

Human Sacrifice (Innovation) (Horror)

Joy Is A Phone Call Away - (A More Perfect Union Charity Anthology)

Holiday

A Peace Offering

Father F'in' Christmas

Love and Pride: Bolder Breed Studios #2

TEASER: JOY IS A PHONE CALL AWAY

Excerpt from Joy Is A Phone Call Away from the charity anthology
A More Perfect Union

Act One

Joy

December 2020

"Joy, you'll close up? You're sure? I just can't talk to another person. I'll literally donate a kidney through my nostril to avoid speaking, I'm that sick of humanity."

Karen was our director of the Atlanta call center for the committee to elect Democrat Warren Johnson, and yes, she was fully aware and encouraging of jokes invoking her name. Mr. Johnson found himself in a run-off election after the emotional November race, and it had been all hands on deck ever since with her leading the team.

"I happen to love humanity," I told Karen, "and I'd be happy to close up shop. I just want to finish three more calls tonight so I can reach my goal."

"Suit yourself. Just be careful leaving."

"Oh don't worry. My brother's on standby to pick me up. He won't let the boogeymen get me."

She muttered something like "ain't the boogie men who worry me," then turned and waved as she went out the door. I was her second or third in command, it depended on the day, so I had the codes to the alarm and locks. And though I was tired, it was almost Christmas, and we'd be closing down until after the holiday. No stone could be left unturned in this important race, and that meant having dozens of conversations with potential voters about the issues that concerned them most.

Next on my list was Irma Santiago. I dialed her number and it rang three times before a screaming woman answered the phone.

"*Callate! El telefono!* Bueno?"

I introduced myself in my barely adept Spanish and she laughed. "English is okay. Can I help you?"

"Yes, I'm calling—"

"Bernardo! Get the dog! El Diablo, that dog! Oy! The roast! He's on the counter!"

"I'm sorry, I seem to have caught you at a bad time—"

"It's always like this," she said with a sigh. "What can I do for you?"

"Well, you've probably heard by now about the run-off election—"

"Ay! Gilberto! You're spilling! Bernardo help him—"

"But you told me to get the dog."

"Bernardo! Oh, I'm sorry, what did you say your name was?"

"I'm Joy, and you sound really busy—"

"It's okay, really. I got five kids and two nephews staying with me and my husband. There's always chaos. Anyway, you were saying?"

I had no idea how parents did it. I thought kids sounded like fun, but then I'd witness a meltdown in a store or a tragedy occur and I'd question my own capacity.

"I'll be quick. I just wanted to see if you had any questions about Warren Johnson, our Democratic candidate for the U.S. Senate? We're checking with voters—"

"He's not that one who was on the Twitter complaining about immigrants—"

"No, ma'am. That was his challenger, John Farmingham." Having one old white guy running against another old white guy, especially one with a similar name, was definitely a problem when working on a campaign. Folks were looking for change, and while it seemed like they weren't getting it with either of these candidates, Warren Johnson had recruited a diverse team to help him win. With control of the senate in the balance, we couldn't disappoint.

"Oh, dios mio, that man boils my blood. I will definitely be voting for whoever is not him."

I chuckled. I'd heard a lot of that phone banking for the presidential election.

"That's wonderful. May I ask whether you plan to vote in person or by mail?"

"In person. I want to look those people in the eye when I deliver my vote."

"Those people?" I asked her. *The poll workers?*

"Those militia people. I saw them there last time with their guns, like they're gonna scare me away from voting. I've worked hard and no one is going to tell me I don't belong here."

"Yes, ma'am. I'm glad to hear it. Do you have any questions for me?"

"What? Jose! Put that down right now! No, you may not eat that candy bar while dinner is cooking!"

Oh, this woman was my hero. She managed to handle a conversation with me while dealing with chaos.

"I'm so sorry, Mrs. Santiago. I'm happy to let you go for the evening."

"It's okay. These kids make me crazy, but they're good boys. Did you need anything else?"

"No, ma'am. Thank you for taking the time to speak with me."

"No, thank you for calling. I can't volunteer, but you sure have my vote."

"Thank you so much. Have a good evening."

We hung up and I made a note on the spreadsheet and then threw my hands up in the air and spun in my chair.

"Winning!"

I loved a good call where I could connect with like-minded people. It gave me faith in humanity. I would often tell Karen she needed to make calls so she could hear from the good ones. I was on such a high from the last call I was dancing in my seat as I dialed the next number.

"This is Dylan."

I was ripped from my moment of glory.

"Uh, I'm sorry, is this Dylan Whitley?"

"Yes it is, may I ask who's calling?"

I wasn't prepared for the soft, sleepy voice on the other end of the line. Leftover assumptions from an era that made them freely.

"Hi, um, hi. Sorry. I'm Joy and I'm calling with the party. The Democrats. The run-off. Oh my god, can I start over?"

The line was dead silent and I thought for sure she'd hung up on me.

Then she chuckled.

"Give it a shot."

"Great. Thank you. I'm not usually this bad."

"Okay."

I'm not sure what I was expecting, but more quiet distracted me again. I found myself trying to picture what Dylan Whitley looked like. What would the face to match that incredible voice be like?

"Are you there?"

Her voice startled me and I jumped, knocking over a cup with push pins, which went all over the floor. I jumped up and smacked my shin on the corner of the desk drawer, which I always did and I specifically reminded myself to watch out for every time I got up. I made a face to keep from shouting and then let out a long breath.

"I'm so sorry. I just...Hi. Let me start over." *Pull it together Joy.* "I'm Joy and I'm calling from the Georgia Democratic Party and I wanted to—"

"The run-off election."

I exhaled for probably the first time since she'd answered.

"Yes. I wanted to ask you if you were planning to vote?"

The line went quiet.

"I'd planned to, but uh...I've had a change of status."

"Oh." I wasn't prepared for that answer, but I was a professional. I could handle it. "Is there something I can help with?"

"Not unless you are a miracle worker."

"Well," I said and then barked out a laugh. "I bring Joy with every call, so miracles aren't too far out of my purview." She'd laugh at my stupid joke, or she'd hang up. Either way, I likely wasn't making a good impression. The dead air on the other end of the line was killing me.

"Do you always work this hard for a laugh?"

"I'll do anything to protect our democracy, so I guess slipping on a banana peel or a bad pun aren't too high a price to pay."

"Duly noted." And she laughed. It felt like a victory.

"I'm serious, is there something I can help with?" I wasn't ready to give up yet.

"We're past the deadline for requesting mail-in ballots, aren't we?"

"We are. Does that mean you're out of the area?"

She cleared her throat and I could have sworn I heard a grunt of pain.

"I am now. I won't be on Election Day, but I likely won't be able to get to the polling place."

"Oh, well, I think I can help with that. I've got charts, graphs, schedules, lists, you name it, all methods of transportation necessary to get you from point A to point Ballot." My fingers twitched over the keyboard as I prepared to wow her with my resourcefulness since my humor hadn't done the trick.

"I'm afraid it's more than a matter of transportation. I'm, uh, disabled."

She said the word as though it were new and unfamiliar.

"That's all right," I said, rushing ahead. "There are paratransits and heck, we can even set up a private ride if you're okay with that."

She sighed.

That wasn't a good sign.

"Well, Joy, I'm *newly disabled*," she said, drawing it out to make a point. "So when I get out of the rehab hospital I'm currently in, I won't be real mobile."

My heart flipped around in my chest. "I'm so sorry. I'm sure that's a big adjustment."

"It is," she said. She said it matter-of-factly but I heard pain in her voice. I pictured her in a hospital bed, the room dark as it was nearing nine o'clock. Maybe she was staring out the window at a lone light in the parking lot wondering what the future had in store for her. More pain? Hard work? Frustration. And yet she was strong enough to talk to a stranger on the phone.

I wasn't sure if she would want to talk to me or feel comfortable sharing her tale with a stranger, but since she hadn't hung up on me yet, I thought perhaps there was a reason fate placed her number on my list for calls tonight.

Joy comes calling January 18, 2021

Please sign up for my newsletter at www.rlmerrillauthor.com to be notified when the anthology goes on sale. All proceeds will go to benefit voter support organizations.

TEASER: LOVE AND PRIDE: A BOLDER BREED STUDIOS F/F HOLIDAY NOVELLA

Feedback Magazine
December 2019

Holidays with Love and Pride: The Magic of Bolder Breed Studios
Krishnan Guruvayoor

What do you get when you cross a multitalented pop ingenue whose star is on the rise, and a veteran producer who walks the edge of mainstream with one foot in the game and the other in a puddle of opaque brilliance? This year, you get a phenomenally refreshing holiday gift. Incognito Records has put together a heartwarming collection of traditional holiday songs recorded by artists who are part of the LGBTQ community. Their goal is to raise money for the #LoveIsLove Foundation, which was started by Reese Matheson and Toby Griffiths when their musical *Boy* came out two years ago. With artists like Just Like Love, Hush, Unice Love, and Backdrop Silhouette on board, the album will be a mix of genres from metal to pop punk to soulful pop, a collaboration unheard of previously in the music industry.

I'll be chatting with all of the artists involved as they share their reasons for participating in this special project and what it was like stepping onto the hallowed grounds of Bolder Breed Studios outside Portland, Oregon.

Unice Love and Lydia Pride have created a masterpiece collaboration for this project comparable to David Bowie and Bing Crosby doing "Little Drummer Boy," or the smash hit from Mariah Carey and Walter Afanasieff, "All I Want for Christmas is You." I've come to the Bolder Breed Studios compound outside of Portland, Oregon, to meet with the pop star and producer. They are currently working on Love's fourth album, which promises to be yet another smash. The unlikely pair—who share they have recently become a pair in work *and* life—took some time to chat with me and explain how they hope their Christmas song will bring solace to those who struggle with the holidays and help change negative attitudes toward the LGBTQ community, which those of you who followed my former blog as The Guru will recognize as a cause near and dear to my heart.

We meet in a dark leather booth in the bar area of the main lodge Lydia Pride calls home. Pride and business partner producer Morrison Jones set up the studio here outside of Portland a few years ago, and not only have they turned it into a thriving community for musicians and artists, but they've built a three-thousand-seat outdoor amphitheater that boasts excellent sound and comfort for guests. Pride and Love have just come from a swim break after working in the studio and the elder stateswoman is making the ingenue squeal by flinging her wet curls at her.

Krish: *Thank you both for agreeing to chat. I hope I'm not interrupting the creative flow.*

Unice: *No, you're good. Lydia is packing to run off and meet up with Alicia Keys anyway.*

She elbows her and Lydia rolls her eyes, but leans in so Unice can kiss her on the cheek. Immediately you can see how they move together, in sync, like a well-oiled machine. Makes me wonder how that translates sonically.

Lydia: *I'm only going to be gone for a week, and then we'll finish recording this album before you leave to go on tour for four months.*

Krish: *I can imagine it would be tough to be apart after you've just found each other. It certainly was for my partner and I.*

Unice: *It is weird, but then I don't think either of us expected this to be anything other than a quick recording session. My label approached me with the idea of covering "Let It Snow" as part of this album to raise funds for the #LoveIsLove Foundation. After everything that happened to me last year, I jumped at the chance to be a part of the project.*

Unice is referring to the attempted shooting at her Miami concert last year. Thankfully, no one was hurt. The resulting trial revealed the depths of the conspiracy behind the attack, which resulted in Unice canceling tour dates and tightening her personal security. It was a scary reminder that there is still hatred toward those who are part of the LGBTQ music community as well as their allies. My partner, metal singer Silas Franklin, and I have experienced this firsthand, but we are blown away by the support we've had as our story has been shared on social media. Unice has emerged from the incident more determined than ever to be a part of positive change and we at Feedback magazine are pleased to support her. It's good to see her strong, confident, and excited about her latest endeavor.

Unice: *When I came up here, I thought that was it. I'd sing the song, and be onto the next thing. Instead I ended up—*

Lydia: *You ended up finding your true voice.*

Unice: *I did, didn't I?*

Lydia: *Look, Unice needs a support team, don't get me wrong, and once we all agreed to play nice, I was able to show Unice that she needed to trust herself in order to shine. She does that just fine on her own.*

Unice: *Mmm-hmm.*

Lydia: *What?*

Unice: *You left out one very important piece. I needed this* place—*and you—to show me what I was capable of, so don't discount that.*

Krish: *So what was it about working with Lydia that turned out to be a game changer for you, Unice? In life and in your career?*

Unice couldn't believe she and Lydia were about to spill the beans to the world the story of how their relationship came to be, but she trusted Lydia, and Lydia had said she trusted Krish, otherwise, she never would have let him into her inner sanctum. Their home.

That was the first lesson Unice learned when she'd arrived at Bolder Breed Studios back in October. Lydia was all about trust, and she definitely had her rules.

October 2019

Unice worried the address her manager Velma had been given was wrong when they'd turned off a highway outside of Portland, Oregon, and pulled up to a brick hotel-looking building. The country road seemed to be leading them straight into the plot of a horror movie, and her nerves weren't eased when they got out of the car and heard only...nature. Unice had never been somewhere so quiet in her entire life. No cars flying by or honking, no helicopters or sirens. Just a blissful breeze blowing through the trees, the crunch of gravel under her shoes, and the occasional call of a bird.

She'd been further convinced they were in the wrong place when they walked into what appeared to be the main building and saw a typical check-in desk, but then a woman dressed in a band tee with a scene hairdo and ripped jeans popped up from behind the counter and hurried over to welcome them.

"Oh hey! Glad you made it."

"Is this Bolder Breed Studios?" Unice asked as Gladys stepped up next to her.

"She's supposed to meet with Lydia Pride," Gladys said with a little more force than necessary. "Is she here?"

"I'm Rose. You must be Unice?"

Unice accepted the hand the woman offered and was eased by her cheerful smile. "I am. And this is my manager Velma and my assistant Gladys."

Rose shook hands with the two women, who were eyeing her suspiciously.

"*This* isn't the studio, but yeah, you're in the right place. Let me show you to your rooms so you can drop off your things, and then I'll take you to Lydia."

Gladys and Velma whispered to each other, but Unice focused on the back of Rose's head as she walked in front of her down the hall. It seemed like the only time Unice wasn't following someone—or someone's agenda, these days—was when she was onstage. The rest of her time was scheduled to the millisecond and guided by someone else.

"I hope your drive down from Seattle wasn't too bad. Traffic can suck." Rose turned and smiled—and slowed down to walk beside Unice.

"It was fine."

"You're a lot farther out of town than I thought you'd be," Velma said. "I was expecting Portland to be..." She gestured around with her two-inch-long, pearl-white acrylic nails as though they might claw the description right out of the air.

"In the twenty-first century, at least," Gladys said, wrinkling her nose at their surroundings. "I feel like we just stepped back in time.

This is some *Grapes of Wrath* kinda place here." The Hoyt sisters had grown up in Los Angeles, as had Unice, and were most comfortable in the city. Portland wasn't quite *city* enough for them, Unice could tell.

"This place used to be a poor home, a place for the unemployed, unhoused, unwanted. The folks we bought it from turned it into a winery, and now we've made it a home for us wayward musicians and artists. We're still updating some of the place, but the rooms have all been modernized. You'll have everything you need to be comfortable for your stay." Rose's smile was confident. Unice got the sense Rose was used to the place being underestimated.

Rose made it a point to answer Gladys's and Velma's questions, but she'd spoken directly to Unice.

This is nice.

Somewhere along the way, Unice had allowed others to speak for her, plan for her, *do* for her. She'd let it happen. After the incident, well, it had just been easier to let everyone take over. It drove her nuts, but she was too conciliatory to speak up. For now.

"Thanks. I love it already. I'm sure it will be great."

Rose pulled out a pile of actual metal keys, antique fancy-looking ones, and sorted them in her hands. "You're staying 'til Sunday? Working with Lydia today and tomorrow, spa treatments Sunday before you take off Monday, that sound right?"

Unice opened her mouth to answer and—

"We'll see how things go," Gladys said. "If Unice isn't comfortable, we may head back to Seattle early."

"I'm sure everything will be great." Unice mustered up a brave, professional smile. "I'm looking forward to being in one place for three nights. I haven't had that in a while."

Rose gave a little pout. "That's gotta be rough. I live here most of the time, but I've traveled a bit with our business partner before, and when he goes, he's *gone*. Whirlwind trips where you can barely remember what day it is, much less where you rested your head the night before."

Unice laughed, and it sounded a little like clearing cobwebs to her. *Did anyone else notice?*

"Baby, we were in Seattle for a week this time." Velma patted Unice's shoulder.

"Yeah, but two different hotels and then a night with my aunt, and—"

"Who knew the first hotel would be so nasty?" Gladys shuddered. "I swear I got bedbugs just stepping in the lobby. You don't have bedbugs here, do you?"

Rose shook her head and handed them each a skeleton key with a heart keychain that had the number on it.

"These rooms each have one bed, so I gave you three right together. I know you requested a suite, but our two suites have been rented long-term, and our two bedrooms were set aside for folks from the wildfires."

"Oh that's so nice of you," Unice said. "The fires have been awful. My parents—"

"Unice, maybe we shouldn't stay here," Velma said. "I know you prefer to room with one of us—"

"It'll be fine," Unice said, a little too forcefully, and Velma's expertly arched eyebrows disappeared under her bangs.

At one time, Unice had been intimidated by the older woman, but once she got to know Velma Hoyt, she understood that her sternness was about protecting her clients' interests, and she appreciated that. She was a tall, curvy Black woman who ran Unice's career like a tight ship, happy to make Unice her sole focus. She and her older sister Gladys left lucrative agency jobs after fifteen years in the music business to work for Unice full time, and Unice was grateful for them both.

"Oh, shoot," Rose said, looking down at her phone. "I forgot to tell Lydia you were here. Let's put your things away and then I can take you to the studio."

"Go ahead, babe," Velma said. "I'll get your stuff settled. You and Gladys can go."

"Lydia is only expecting Unice. She's very particular about who she lets into the studio. And no cell phones." Rose's smile never wavered, but her voice was firm.

Unice felt bad for her if she was going to challenge Velma and Gladys. She was lucky to have the best manager and assistant in the business, even if they were a little—okay, a lot—overbearing.

Velma and Gladys exchanged looks and then turned and faced Rose, shoulder to shoulder. "Thank you. We'll just take a minute with Unice and then we'll be ready to go to the studio." Velma put a hand on Unice's shoulder and guided her into the middle room of the three they'd been given the keys to.

Unice glanced over her shoulder with an apologetic smile for Rose.

Rose didn't seem ruffled at all. "No prob. I'll be up at the front desk. Come on over when you're ready."

"Thank you," Unice called out.

Gladys closed the door and turned to face her. "Unice, are you okay with this? I'm not sure how I feel about sending you in alone. Are you okay without your cell phone?"

Unice turned around in the center of the simple but clean room. The walls were covered with a tan wallpaper and green wainscoting. Large windows let in ample sunlight across the white duvet and dark wood floor covered with a bright multi-colored rug. The en suite bathroom was neat and tidy with a large walk-in shower. She smiled at her handlers. She appreciated their protectiveness, but she felt positive about this place. It wasn't fussy or too modern. It felt like staying at a relative's house. "I'm fine. I like it. It's peaceful here. Fewer distractions."

Gladys crossed her arms over her chest. "It's the boonies out here. I don't like that we're not in the same room. I'm sure it's safe enough, but with things the way they are, I'm just concerned."

Unice sighed. She hated being reminded.

She released her first solo album after three years on the teenage-friendly hit show *Advantageous* and from the beginning she decided that she was going to be very open about her sexual orientation. She didn't want any coming-out scandals, and so she'd deliberately let people know through her actions and her interviews and conversations that she was gay, although she'd been discreet with her few dating experiences.

She'd received death threats on her last tour from a hate group, so she'd hired a private security firm. The group members had taken offense to her videos that prominently featured members of the LGBTQ community, and they posted that she should stay out of things like civil rights and the Black Lives Matter movement and focus on being an entertainer. Then an FBI investigation uncovered a plot for gunmen to take over her show in Miami. They caught the suspects coming into the arena and neutralized the threat before anyone was hurt, but it was too close for comfort. They arrested three men on-site and two for the online threats, and she'd had to testify at the trial. It had been a harrowing experience, and since then, she never went anywhere alone. This was the first trip she and the Hoyt sisters had taken without her personal bodyguard in a long time. The label assured them that Bolder Breed's compound was a secure, safe place. Stephenee was on call just in case. Unice hoped they didn't have to bother her.

"We'll put you between us at least," Velma said. "I'm a light sleeper. I'll hear if anything happens."

"I'm sure it will be fine," Unice said. She really wanted life to get back to some semblance of normal, and this trip was a first step. Velma and Gladys both had advanced belts in Kajukenbo. The three of them trained together with her fitness coach, Randy Ramos, in LA. So she felt safe-ish.

She walked over to the window and looked outside. There was a large fountain in the middle of the driveway, and the sound of the water was soothing. If it weren't so chilly outside, she'd have loved to open her window and listen all night. Open windows overnight, however, were a no-no.

"I'll put your stuff down here, okay, honey?"

"Thank you. I just...I need...a minute."

Her two gatekeepers stared for a moment, looked at each other, and then left the room, closing the door behind them.

Velma and Gladys had this way of staring at her as if she might break. She *had* broken. But she'd been doing so much better. And this trip was one she'd actually been excited about. She'd wanted to work with Lydia Pride ever since she'd heard her collaboration with Dolly Parton on the music for a recent YA film on Netflix. Then she looked up some of the other artists Lydia produced: Courtney Love, Lady Gaga, Alicia Keys...she had a wide reach when it came to pop music, and her songs were identifiable in that they tended to be departures from those artists' main collections of songs.

Unice wanted departure.

She wanted to go deeper, wanted to do more than be the airheaded, sheltered, performing puppet her critics thought she was. She wanted to write her own songs, wanted to stop relying on stage shows, skimpy outfits, and shaking her ass to sell records. Wanted to prove she was more than just a teen television star, more than a pretty face with a decent voice.

But there were roadblocks and complications in the way of her plans. She owed the label another album soon, and they'd expect a certain sound. They were lining up producers without her input, and she had more tour dates scheduled after the first of the year. And now she had this charity album to contribute to.

Okay, she *was* excited about singing a holiday song.

She was a huge geek for Christmas. Ever since she was a kid, her family had some serious holiday traditions. Her mom had freaked out when she'd told her she would be contributing to this charity project without even knowing what song Unice would be singing. Her grandparents were totally thrilled. She got a little warm, fuzzy feeling when she thought about it being a part of her story, her legacy; that she would someday be able to share the song with her children and grandchildren.

She'd been staring out the window long enough. It was time to meet Lydia Pride.

Unice was determined to play this right. She wanted to learn from this woman; she wanted to create the best song she could.

She needed to prove that she was a grown-ass woman, and she was going to take charge and—

"Unice! Come on, honey. You don't want to keep her waiting." Gladys and Velma stood in her doorway, looking around at her room, probably noticing that she hadn't moved.

"Sorry. Give me one second."

Velma raised her eyebrows and closed the door again.

Unice took a quick second to use the restroom and then she hurried out to the hallway. She'd wanted to change out of her traveling clothes—black and white floral palazzo pants and a matching black long-sleeved, fitted top with cutouts on her side and shoulder —and fix her long rose-gold ponytail, but she'd wasted her few precious moments to herself staring out the window. Her light-brown skin could use some sun, her large brown eyes, probably her best feature, were a tad puffy, but she'd left the makeup off hoping it would go away.

No more stalling. It was time to take that first step toward being her own boss.

"Here, let me fix your hair," Gladys said, whipping out her brush and pulling Unice to a stop by her ponytail. "You've got wispies."

"You sure you don't want to change?" Velma pulled out her phone and checked her itemized list for the day. "Did you take your supplements this morning? I forgot to ask you at breakfast. We'll have to let Lydia know that you have to take a break at eleven forty-five to stretch and then eat lunch. We don't want that back spasm coming back."

Unice sighed as tears stung her eyes. Of course, those could have been from the force Gladys used to yank her curly hair into submission. She knew better than to pull away. Her baby fine hair was tough to manage and despite having a tender head, she sat for braids, extensions, up dos, whatever her stylist suggested and tried her best to keep from crying. She'd gotten the hairbrush plenty of times growing up from her aunties and mom, and even though she was twenty-five years old, you never forget that feeling.

"There. Oh, I should have brought my makeup kit. Well, you look fabulous, and from what I've seen of this lady," she said out the side of her mouth, "she's not about fashion."

Okay, maybe she would be her own boss...later.

www.ingramcontent.com/pod-product-compliance
Lightning Source LLC
Chambersburg PA
CBHW030600130626
46552CB00006B/2610